The Lucky Place

The Lucky Place

Zu Vincent

Mishawaka-Penn-Harris
Public Library
Mishawaka, Indiana

ACKNOWLEDGMENTS

Several talented people have championed this novel. It's a privilege to work with my editor, Joy Neaves, and the Front Street staff; my agent, Erin Murphy; and the extraordinary Carolyn Coman.

I'd like to thank Vermont College and its fine community of writers for their encouragement and support, including the wise pros Jacqueline Woodson, Jane Resh Thomas, Tim Wynne-Jones, M.T. Anderson, Marc Aronson, Margaret Bechard, and Laura Kvasnosky. Special thanks to Elizabeth Bluemle and the Flying Pig Bookstore.

I owe a long-standing debt to the many passionate readers and writers in California and the support offered from writers' groups in San Francisco, Sacramento, Santa Cruz, Squaw Valley, and the Chico area. Thanks as well to the Iowa Writers' Workshop.

I'm forever grateful to fellow writers Barb, Debbie, Rose, Tami, and Vicki for their friendship and laughter, and to Ann for always loving this story. Thank you, Laurie, for being in my world. And my love and awe to my gifted first readers and family, the artists Harry, Kiara, and Aubrie.

Library of Congress Cataloging-in-Publication Data

Vincent, Zu.
The lucky place / Zu Vincent. — 1st ed.
p. cm.
Summary: In the 1970s, a girl comes of age struggling with the loss
of two father figures in her life.
ISBN 978-1-932425-70-3 (hardcover : alk. paper)
[1. Fathers and daughters—Fiction. 2. Coming of age—Fiction.] I. Title.
PZ7.V7453Lu 2008
[Fic]—dc22
2007018357

Front Street
An Imprint of Boyds Mills Press, Inc.
815 Church Street
Honesdale, Pennsylvania 18431

for H.K.
and in memory of
Vince and John Mark

Part 1

"So sad, too bad, your dad."
—*Old Daddy*

At the Races

There are always secrets.

"Mum's the word," says Daddy. "We were never at the races." He has hold of our hands and we're standing in a mash of people. He lets go to drink from the secret skinny bottle he keeps inside his coat. His eyes crinkle at the edges, and he pushes his hat way back on his head and pulls it forward again.

Daddy's hair is curly black and his eyes are very blue. He calls me Baby Doll. Jamie is his little man. Jamie's hair is curly black and his eyes are very blue, too. Daddy says Jamie can charm the pants off a snake. I can't charm the pants off a snake.

"This here's my little girl, this here's my Baby Doll," says Daddy to the man with fat gold buttons.

"Hello," the man says, but I don't talk back. I go way inside where he can't reach me. "Baby Doll, same as the horse," he says. He pinches my cheek and laughs. "Cat got your tongue?" he asks.

Daddy gives money to the lady with the fence in front of her face to put on Baby Doll. Then we climb the big stairs to sit on hard, sunny benches. Daddy's getting his floppy smile, the one that makes him friends. His friends crowd all around us. They thump his back. They laugh when he laughs.

He shakes everybody's hand. "How de do," he says, "name's Sikes." He pushes his hat back on his head and tips his secret skinny bottle way up in the sky to get it all. Then he pulls his hat back down.

Jamie is five, so he's too big, but I can sit on Daddy's lap. I put my hands on Daddy's cheeks where the little hairs poke out. He kisses me wet and squeezes. I feel in my coat pocket for my ticket to the races. It's long and smooth and a horse runs across one end. There are more tickets like this on the floor by Daddy's feet, because people throw them there and step on them. I look around to see if any of the other tickets are still good enough to save, but none of them are as nice as mine.

There's nothing else to do. The sun gets hot and Daddy takes my coat off. I've got my Sunday-school dress underneath. Daddy lights a Chesterfield. His silver lighter clicks open and the flame pops up. He asks his friends if it isn't a thirsty day, and they say yes, it's a thirsty day, so he buys them grown-up drinks. Jamie begs for hot dogs and Cokes.

A giant voice above our heads calls the names of the horses lining up. Daddy tells me to stand on the seat to see them. The bell rings and the horses run. They kick up dust. All the people shout together, but Daddy's shouts are loudest. "Go, Baby Doll, go!" he yells, and his veins swell big in his neck.

It doesn't take as long for the horses to race as it does to wait for them. All they do is run around the big track and back again. When they're done Daddy jumps up and down and hugs us.

"She did it! She did it!" he shouts. He bumps my hot dog and spills ketchup on my dress, but he doesn't care. "Stay here while I collect," Daddy says.

Jamie sits on the bench, but I shake my head. "No, no, no," I say. I hug Daddy's neck. I don't want him to leave us. Daddy rubs his pokey cheek. He tries to unhook my arms, only I hang on good, so he has to pick me up and take me with him.

There are a hundred people where we collect. They stand in more long lines and push. Daddy sets me down and I can't see anything. I have to hold very tight to his hand. I let go when he gets his money. Then I grab his hand back.

Jamie has our places saved on the sunny bench. He makes Daddy's new friends move over. He has to yell and shove.

"We're rich," Daddy says. "We made a killing." He waves the dollars for his friends to see. "Good ol' Baby Doll," he says. "I knew it'd be Baby Doll."

Daddy's friends crowd in. They ask Daddy if he isn't thirsty again, and Daddy says he's always thirsty, so they buy him more grown-up drinks. They watch him count his money. They whisper in his ear. Pretty soon Daddy's holding out his money. "Take some, Tom," he says, "Mike. We made a killing, didn't we make a killing, Baby Doll?" And Tom and Mike take some of Daddy's money.

We stand up and sit down for the horses so many times that Daddy's friends are leaving. Jamie doesn't have to shove to keep our places anymore. "We're just betting now," Daddy says. "Betting that we back another winner." My legs get tired, but I still want to go with Daddy down the stairs and into the mash of people.

This time the stairs seem like forever. At the bottom the people are a bunch of legs and hands. Daddy walks like a hay-wire toy. He's lost his floppy smile. I try to keep his hand, but it moves too fast and gets away.

"Daddy!" I yell. "Daddy!" I grab his coat edge. Daddy's coat jerks one way and then the other. It flies out of my fingers so I can't get it back. It disappears between the legs and hands, and Daddy's swallowed up.

Beer for Breakfast

Mama lets me sleep with her when Gold Buttons brings me home from the races. She lays in the big bed and holds me extra tight. She smells like lipstick, grown-up drink, and the secret things in her top drawer. "My baby," she whispers, "my baby," and smooths my hair. She smooths and smooths until it feels like that place in my head will have a crease in the morning. But I don't tell her to stop. Mama's crying.

"I'll kill him," she says. "I will." Her grown-up drink has melty ice and makes wet circles on the table. She rolls the glass on her forehead. She leaves the light burning.

I don't want Mama to kill Daddy. I shut my eyes and pretend I never let go, that I held on tight to Daddy, so he could bring me home like he brought Jamie. I'm hot with Mama's arms around me. Then I'm cold. I'm falling through the cold and I land in a hard place where she's covering me up. I hear her slippers soft on the floor, her shushy gown. I see my clown-face night-light and the crack of light at the door. The light stretches and Mama's inside it. She stands so long it's like her face is pressing into mine. Pressing how she does when my forehead is hot.

I must be dreaming. I dream a crash and Mama yells through the wall.

"How could you, Sikes!" screams Mama. "How could you?"

"Honey, please calm down."

I roll over in my bed. I scrunch under the covers, and my hands fit down between my knees. I squeeze my eyes shut. I think that's Daddy talking.

But in the morning, Daddy isn't home. Aunt Larue is in the kitchen, watching Mama pick up dishes. Mama walks back and forth, tossing dishes in the sink, and the dishes bang. "The last straw and I mean it," Mama says.

Jamie and I spread Lincoln Logs on the living room rug. We watch Aunt Larue's skinny back and Mama moving near the sink. "Let's make a fort," Jamie whispers. He lays out four logs for the square.

"Slow down, Belle," says Aunt Larue. "You're making me dizzy." Aunt Larue's voice is crackly when she talks. She takes a sip of beer. Beer is brown in tall bottles and makes your tongue flinch. "Don't ever get to liking it," she says when I make a face. "Especially not for breakfast." But Jamie asks for another taste.

Mama can't slow down. Her hands go this way and that. They crawl up her throat; they poke her hair. "What am I doing here? What am I doing?" she says. She scrubs the dishes. She looks out the window at our brown old grass. "I've got to turn my luck around."

"He's just laying low. He'll straighten up." The beer makes Aunt Larue burp.

Mama grabs Aunt Larue's beer and takes a drink. "And what if he doesn't?"

"You've got two kids," says Aunt Larue.

"So do you, and you left Sam."

"Sam left me. You don't want to be alone."

Mama slaps the beer bottle down. Her face is pink and shiny. "I won't ever be alone," she says.

"What are you saying? Does *he* still call?"

"Shhh." Mama looks over at me and Jamie, and she and Aunt Larue start to whisper.

The fort gets higher. Jamie lets me pick out the red pieces for the roof. "I lost Daddy," I tell him. "I couldn't hold on."

13

"That's because you're little." Jamie helps me put the red pieces on straight. He can make the fort look good. "I would've stayed right with him."

"It's not because I'm little," I say. "Daddy went too fast."

"Don't cry. Want me to dance for you?" Jamie jumps up. He taps his feet across the floor, heel-toe, heel-toe, and his dancing makes me smile.

Laying Low

You two better straighten up and fly right, Mama tells us when we're bad. Now Daddy's bad, too, and I close my eyes and wish and wish for him to straighten up. When he's laying low, Mama's mad, Jamie has a sorry face, and I don't know what to do. All day I listen for Daddy's step outside. His jingly keys. "Come away from the window," Mama says at bedtime. "He's not coming back." The way she says this makes me think she doesn't want him to.

She lets us stay in her bed. She reads to us from the book with the leathery-smelling pages. The book pictures have no frames but walk around the printed stories, bright and deep, until you fall into them.

"Things are changing," Mama says when the story is over. "I want you kids to be extra good."

"I will," I promise, but I feel funny. What things? What's changing? I don't want things to change. The phone rings and Mama hurries to get it. Jamie hasn't promised to be extra good. He follows and pulls on her skirt, but Mama says, "It's not Daddy." Then she turns away and whispers.

"Call Daddy," Jamie begs when she hangs up. "Tell him to come home."

"I can't. He's gone to work," Mama says. "He's out of town." A salesman doesn't work in any one place. He drives around. He talks to people. "Your daddy could sell anything to anybody," Mama says. "He's a regular charm-boy. Jamie, you get that from him." The way she says this I can't tell if it's good or not.

Daddy doesn't come back and he doesn't come back. Mama calls Aunt Larue to stay with us while she works. Aunt Larue is a sourpuss and makes us pull Mama's green chair against the door when Mama leaves. "Nobody's safe on the south side," says Aunt Larue. "That's why your mama wants out."

Ellis

Mama has a day off. She takes forever combing her hair and making her fingernails pointy red. She wears her church suit even though it's not Sunday. She rushes us. She says Jamie and I have to dress up too, so we can get our picture.

I don't like dressing up. I have to wear the new white hat that looks big as a plate with blue ribbons around the edge. Those ribbons are exactly the color of the blue ribbons on my dress. The dress is scratchy and has an extra dress on top that Mama calls a pinafore. There's more blue in my socks turned over at the ankles and edged with lace, and my shoes are shiny black.

I don't want to have my picture in this dress. I shake my head when Mama holds it out. I won't step in.

"Cassie," Mama says. "You're wearing it. I worked hard to

buy this dress. I never had a dress of my own at your age. I only had old hand-me-downs."

I look at Mama. She has black stuff on her eyes and red red lipstick. Her hair is a color she calls auburn. "Gentlemen prefer blondes, they marry brunettes, but the whole world loves a redhead," Mama says. I don't know what old hand-me-downs are.

Mama grabs my shoulders. Her hands shake but her voice is soft. "Sweetheart, please be good," she says. "And we might get a new daddy."

"But where's our old daddy?" I say. "Why isn't he coming back?"

Mama blinks and a tear comes out. She wipes it away with her handkerchief.

My stomach squeezes. "Mama," I say, "do we have to get a new daddy because I lost the old one at the races?"

"Don't be silly, Cass," says Mama. "It started long before that." She kisses me quick and calls for Jamie to hurry.

I have to walk careful in the hat or it tips to the side, and I have to step big onto the curb so I don't get a mark on the toes of my shoes. They hurt my feet, but they smell good. Like the box and the whispering paper and like something else, too.

"I could have got tap shoes instead," Jamie says about his new blue suit. "Real ones made from patent leather." When he grows up he wants to dance like Fred Astaire.

"Someday," Mama says. "How do I look?" I think she looks pretty, but she isn't sure. She stops under a tree in the big black parking lot. The parking lot is sunny and hurts to look at. We wait while she pokes at her hair and pulls her jacket straight even though it's already straight. She opens her purse and takes a little mirror out so she can see to put on more red lipstick.

16

Watching Mama, I touch my hat to tell if it's crooked. I promise myself to be extra good. I wonder if we're going to find our new daddy in the store. I want to ask Jamie, but he runs ahead of us across the parking lot. "Jamie!" Mama yells. "Look both ways!" And she grabs my hand and pulls me across too, and into the dark, cool store. I can't see anything for a while until my eyes unfuzz.

"Don't ever do that again." Mama catches Jamie by the door. "You could have been run over."

"No, I couldn't. I looked."

"Listen to me. Stay right with me." Mama wears gloves that come off one finger at a time. She pulls and pulls and looks around. A man is waving to us. He's tall and has slicked-back hair and a little black mustache.

"Who are you?" Jamie asks when he comes over.

Mama laughs like something is funny. "This is Ellis, from work." Mama's work is being a waitress at El Rancho restaurant. She puts her cheek against the man's cheek. She looks right in his eyes. "Here they are," she says about us. She laughs again.

"Hello, Jamie." Ellis smiles. "You must be the five-year-old." Ellis's hand goes over his slicked-back hair. Then he shakes Jamie's hand.

Jamie stares at him. He doesn't smile back.

Ellis wears a tie like a big shoestring around his neck, and a black stone on the tie. He doesn't wear a hat like Daddy, but he smokes a pipe. He puffs and bends his knees until his face fits in front of my face. He takes my hand and shakes it, too.

"Hello, Cassie," he says. "Almost four, right?" I don't know how he knows our names and ages.

"Aren't you going to say hello?" Mama's nails pinch my back. "She's shy," she says when I don't say anything.

Ellis nods. "That's okay. I have a little girl as shy as you. And Jamie, I have a boy your age. Someday you can meet them."

His eyes have little happy lights in them. He doesn't say the cat got my tongue. If we're going to pick a new daddy here, I'd like this one. But if he already has a little girl like me and a boy like Jamie, how can he be our daddy?

"After your picture," Ellis says, "would you like to ride the elephant?" My stomach squeezes. I don't know what elephant he means. He stands back up until he's way taller than Mama.

Mama says, "Oh, Ellis, she's too little."

"Are you too little?" he asks.

"I'm not too little," Jamie says. "But it isn't real."

"Sure it's real," Ellis says. "He's over in front of JC Penney." One of his eyes squinches down without the other one. Jamie calls this a wink.

Riding the Elephant

After our picture we walk to see the elephant. I keep thinking about Ellis's little girl and boy. Jamie holds Mama's hand and won't let go. He doesn't run ahead. I walk next to Ellis. "Don't stare, Cass," Mama whispers, but I can't help it. I've never picked a new daddy before.

We find a bunch of people and Ellis looks over their heads and says the elephant isn't here yet. He gives the ticket man money and takes two tickets. He holds them out to Jamie and me.

"It isn't real," Jamie says again. He looks funny at me when

I take a ticket. Mama takes the other one when Jamie won't touch it. Jamie nudges me and goes over and shows the ticket man how he can dance like Fred Astaire.

"You want to join the circus?" the ticket man asks, and Mama hears and grabs Jamie to make him stop.

"The elephant's coming," Ellis says. "Who wants to see?" His hands go big around my middle and swing me up. I land on top of his shoulder, which makes me giggle. From here I can look over all the people's heads.

Jamie's wrong. The elephant is real. He's taller than any of the cars and taller than the parking-lot trees. He's got flappy ears and a big snake nose. He's wearing baskets on his back. Children sit in the baskets, with the bottoms of their shoes sticking out.

The elephant gets bigger and bigger. His feet are round and hairy and his skin is extra. His nose curls up and falls down. His tiny eyes look backwards. A man walks beside him and holds a stick in his hand and taps the elephant's foot. The man's not half as tall as the elephant.

When the elephant walks close, Mama yanks Jamie back. The man shouts and the elephant kneels down so he can take the children out.

Jamie is mad that Ellis is right. "I'm not going!" he shouts, and Mama's face gets red. Once the basket is empty, new children get in.

"Jamie," Mama says, "Ellis already bought your ticket."

"No." Jamie shakes his head.

Ellis swoops me down from his shoulder. "How about you, Cassie?" His eyes have the little happy lights in them.

I look at the children climbing in the baskets. "Yes," I say.

Mama makes her surprised face. "Not without Jamie!" she says. "Jamie, take her hand." Only Jamie won't. I think he's scared. But I'm not scared. I want to ride the elephant. When Mama tries to take my ticket back I hold on tight.

"I want to ride the elephant!" I say.

"You won't be able to hang on by yourself," says Mama.

"I can hang on," I tell her.

And Ellis says, "Let her, Belle. It's safe."

"You promise to hang on?" Mama shakes me. She waits. She smells so good I want to hug her neck.

"I promise," I say. I run for the elephant and the elephant man scoops me up and tucks me in the basket. I want Jamie to look at me, but he won't—he watches his shoes. And Mama's eyes are stuck on Ellis.

The elephant man pulls a belt tight around me. I stick my hands on the basket. My blue dress crinkles. The sleeves pinch tight around the tops of my arms. Mama remembers to look now. She asks the elephant man if he's sure the strap will hold, but the elephant's already going up.

I never thought before what an elephant smells like. I never thought before how high you would be on an elephant's back. The basket moves like it might fall off, first one way, then the other, every time the elephant steps.

My stomach is red ribbons. I think about falling all that way. I can see the tops of cars and trees. My tiny Mama acts like she wants me back right now, except it's too late.

"Hang on!" she screams, but it's windy up here. The wind grabs my hat and I have to let go of the basket to save it. Mama's mouth falls open. She hides her face in Ellis's shoulder, which I've never seen her do with anyone but Daddy before.

20

I set the hat safe in my lap. The place for my head stands up round and flat as a birthday cake. When Mama lights the candles she says, "Don't blow them out until you make a wish." I wish we could have this new daddy—then it wouldn't be so bad that I lost our old one at the races.

Pretty soon Mama and Ellis grow tinier and tinier until I can't see them anymore. And it's like losing Daddy, only different, because I'm the one going away.

When the Milk Ran Dry

Daddy comes back smelling bad. Jamie and I run out of bed and stand by the chair until his eyes find us. "So sad, too bad, your dad," he says in his funny voice. "Tough titty said the kitty when the milk ran dry."

Jamie giggles. I tell Daddy I'm sorry I lost him at the races. "Go back to bed," Mama says. She helps Daddy out of his chair and he walks like the haywire toy, down the hall to the bathroom. He bumps into the wall where the copper plate hangs, the one with the ship sailing away. Mama grabs the ship and tries to hold Daddy up. "In your room, now!" she tells us.

Daddy's face is scary, hanging down.

Jamie waits until Mama has got Daddy in the bathroom. Then he sneaks back along the hallway to the bathroom door. I sneak behind him. Mama pushes the door shut, but it doesn't close tight. We can see her and Daddy between the crack.

Daddy's on the toilet seat. Mama bends over the tub. The pipes bang when she turns the faucet. She kneels on the rug.

"Take these off," she says, and I hear Daddy's shoes hit

the floor. "Oh, no!" Mama sounds mad when she pulls down Daddy's pants.

"I'm sorry, honey." Daddy's hand tries to touch Mama's face. It moves around like he can't see. Jamie looks at me and plugs his nose. Daddy has messed his pants like a baby.

Gotcha

A rock pushes against my face. I don't know why I should be sleeping on it. I open my eyes and Jamie's bed sags, so I know he's up there. His mattress is held above mine by wire; if the wire breaks he'll fall on me. I roll over and the rock is only Mama's empty powder box, the see-through one with little grooves on top. That's where I keep my tickets, the ones from the races and the elephant ride. I stand up and poke at Jamie's mattress.

Mama is in her robe in the kitchen, frying bacon. She jabs the fork into the pan, jabs and jabs. Her hair has yellow around it from the window sun. The bacon pops. "Jamie, Cassie, go wake your daddy," she says. "Wait!" she says. "Remember our secret? Both of you?"

We aren't supposed to tell Daddy about Ellis giving us a ticket to ride the elephant. Mama says never take that ticket out of her powder box. Never mention Ellis's name. She says it's on the Q.T., which is another word for secret. "Just give Daddy a kiss," she says.

Jamie and I tiptoe into Mama and Daddy's room. It's dark with the curtains shut. We sneak up to the bed. Daddy's hair curls black around his head. His hand with the big gold ring is still. "Daddy! Daddy!" we call, then jump back. Daddy grabs at Jamie, but he catches me.

"Gotcha!" Daddy growls. Jamie screams and runs away.

"Help! Help!" I say. Daddy pulls me smash against his pokey cheek, and my heart beats fast.

"I can't tell," I say. "Ellis is a secret!" Daddy lets go and stares.

Daddy stays in his room with the door shut. Mama whispers on the phone. I hide under the table holding my ballerina doll, the one with pointy toes and clicky eyes, and when she goes to sleep her eyes fall shut. Daddy comes out with his hanging-down face and pulls the phone away. Mama wants the phone back, but Daddy won't give it. He puts it to his ear.

"Sikes, don't." Mama tries to grab it.

"Who is this?" Daddy asks. He waits. Then he slams the phone down. "Was it him?"

"Who? What are you talking about?"

"Cassie told me, Belle. You think you're in love with that damn cook. Where's my Chesterfields?" Daddy's fingers shake.

"What did Cassie tell you?" Mama says. I cover my ears when I hear my name.

"I don't want him around my kids, damn it."

Mama starts to yell. "And you're so much better? Look at you. You're either sick or off on a binge. We haven't seen you in weeks."

Daddy shakes worse. He finds his Chesterfields. He opens his lighter and the flame pops up. "They're my kids. Not his. They need their old man."

"Sober," Mama says.

"You've made up your mind, haven't you? Just like that. You want to go off with that damn cook." Daddy sounds sad.

Nobody says anything until Mama says, "I just want a family, Sikes."

My ballerina doll goes to sleep and her eyes fall shut. I lay down with her and my stomach squeezes. I just want a family, too.

The Snake

Mama's at work. Daddy is watching us. He watches us from the couch, lying down. Jamie has a Dennis the Menace I'm not allowed to touch. But Jamie is outside and Dennis is on the floor. He isn't wearing his little jeans. I look for the jeans and find them under Jamie's Indian blanket, the one with the cowboys sitting around campfires and the Indians sneaking up on them. I hold Dennis and try to dress him. I stick my fingers in his tiny pockets, which go down like real pockets. I wish I had some tiny money to put in there.

Jamie can sneak up on me faster than anything. He grabs Dennis before I even have the pants half on. Dennis flies up, up above my head, way on top of Jamie's arm where I can't reach.

"Please!" I beg Jamie. I pull on his shirt.

Jamie jiggles Dennis and says, "Trade. I get to play with your ballerina doll."

"No."

"She's mine until tomorrow."

"When's tomorrow?"

"Tomorrow is tomorrow, you dope. The day after today. And I can do her hair and take her tutu off."

Jamie loves her clicky eyes and pointy toes. He loves how her hair is pink and her tutu is pink and so are her shiny slippers and tights. He gives me Dennis the Menace and I hand him my ballerina doll.

"Put her down," says Daddy from the doorway. "That's a girl's doll, Jamie. Boys aren't supposed to play with ballerina dolls."

"Mama lets me."

"Mama isn't here."

After Daddy says this, Jamie cries, in the bathroom where Daddy can't hear. Only I know. I press my ear to the door when Daddy falls asleep on the couch.

"Jamie," I say. "You can have her. I won't tell. Don't cry, Jamie. Come out."

"Go away," says Jamie.

I wait. I don't know what else to do when he won't play with me. I lay on the floor by the door. I try to see under the crack. I listen. I shove my fingers in, and the pink ballerina doll's feet. The floor is hard and cool. My fingers get stuck and they hurt when I pull them out.

The door swings back and Jamie is there. "I don't want that stupid doll," he says. "Come on."

Outside the paint is a color called aqua. Daddy is supposed to put it on the garage walls, only he never does. Jamie opens the paint and sticks the brushes in. One for me and one for him. The way he looks at me I know we aren't supposed to do this.

We paint the neighbor lady's dog. Jamie holds her while I paint her, and I hold her while Jamie does. Her name is Trixie and she's usually fluffy white. Trixie stands still and her tongue droops down. She doesn't move until Daddy comes out.

Daddy is tall on the step. His face is sour and has dents in it from sleeping. He holds a snake in his hand. He comes down the step and the snake goes for Jamie. Jamie screams and the snake goes *Crack. Crack. Crack. Crack.*

"Don't, Daddy! Don't, Daddy!" I shout. I watch Daddy's hand. Daddy stops and looks at me. He blinks like he just woke up. He sits hard on the step. The snake doesn't move. It doesn't look like a snake now. It looks like his alligator belt. But I'm still afraid it will change.

Jamie has run into the yard. Daddy is on the step. He looks sorry at Jamie and he looks sorry at me and he sits and sits.

I think Daddy must be frozen.

Straight Man

"When you were little," Daddy tells me, "my sister tried to steal you. She picked you up and wouldn't let go. She was walking out the door. 'This is the prettiest baby I've ever seen,' she said. 'Just like a baby doll. If I thought I could have me a baby as pretty as this one, I'd go on home and have her.'"

His voice is big in my ear. I fit on his lap and he holds my legs out straight to help my pigeon toes go away. I move when he moves. "Look at me!" Jamie calls. He does his heel-toe across the floor.

Daddy laughs. "You and me, we'll go on the road. A song-and-dance team, Jamie."

"Time for church." Mama comes out of the bedroom all

dressed up. Daddy looks at her. He looks at Jamie dancing.

"You're my kids," he says, "forever and ever."

I pull on Daddy's tie and ask what I'll do on the road.

"You'll be my straight man," Daddy says. I don't know what a straight man is. "He makes people laugh at the funny guy," says Daddy. He walks my legs in the air with his two big hands, faster and faster. His voice goes tiny. "Pigeon toes, pigeon toes," he says, "don't run away from me." But I can't stop my feet from running, sitting still.

After church the sun comes out and Mama gets the camera. Daddy wears his good tan suit and tie. Mama wears her white dress with the collar that looks like wings. Jamie has a suit like Daddy's, only smaller, and I'm in the blue scratchy dress.

Mama holds the camera at her waist and looks inside. I don't see how this works, how it could be looking at the ground and see the three of us, but Mama says she just can't get Daddy's head. Daddy scrunches until he's only as big as Jamie. He puts me and Jamie on his knees.

"Smile," Mama says.

"Smile!" Daddy says.

Daddy's cheek on mine is not pokey now, but soft. His arm is tight around me. He kisses wet, he squeezes.

"Their clothes," Mama shouts, "their good clothes!" But it's too late. Daddy has started to rock. I try to pull away, but he won't let go. Jamie kicks and wiggles. He laughs. Daddy and I are laughing, too. My stomach is red ribbons. I'm looking at the sky, rolling on the wet grass, over and over in Daddy's arms.

The Last Straw

"This is the last straw, and I mean it," Mama says on the phone to Aunt Larue. "He's off on another binge. My kids deserve something better."

I want to tell Mama I don't care. I don't need anything better. I don't need another daddy. But Daddy says you can't tell Mama anything once she's made up her mind.

I wonder what a binge is. I wonder if it's something you can ride, like a plane or a train, or maybe an elephant. I want to ask Daddy, but this time when he goes away he doesn't come back, and that's a secret, too.

Fire

"Fire!" hollers Aunt Larue and she goes running. Down the back porch steps and past the sandbox and the door to the garage where Mama's wringer-washer sits. She goes all the way to the back gate, which we are not supposed to open. Behind the gate is a hidey road that Mama calls an alley. Bad things happen in alleys, Mama says.

Aunt Larue yanks at the gate and the gate falls open. She rushes into a big black cloud. Jamie and I rush after her.

Now I can see a fire truck and a little house with its windows on fire. The house has a door that opens right in the alley, and the alley is full of people. Firemen squirt the fiery house and more black smoke shakes out. Then they clomp inside.

"Oh, my God," says Aunt Larue when the firemen come back out. They are carrying something long and white and covered with a blanket. When they set the long thing down, the blanket falls away. A man who is not a man lies there. He has staring eyes and no hair and his skin is blotchy. He makes my heart bang as hard as the bathroom pipes.

"Don't look!" yells Aunt Larue, and pulls at us until we're back inside the fence.

River City

Mama comes home and hugs me close. She combs my hair. She kisses me, and her red lipstick stays waxy on my cheek. "River City," she says, and the way she says it I can hear the swirly water. She holds a newspaper out for Aunt Larue.

"Way out there? It's nothing but fields." Aunt Larue squinches her face and slaps the newspaper down.

"Not for long." Mama laughs at Aunt Larue and takes the newspaper back. "Town is moving that way. They're going to put in a freeway and stores."

I wiggle on her lap. I wipe my lipstick cheek. I want to hear her laugh again.

"Is there a river, Mama?" I ask.

"There'll be other children to play with," Mama says.

I look for a river in the picture, but I don't see one. "I want to see the river," I say.

"There are no buses out there." Aunt Larue shakes her head at Mama. "You'd have to drive a car." Aunt Larue doesn't know how to drive, but Mama says she doesn't mind, she just needs a car to drive.

"I'd drive to hell and back to live in a place with no alleys," Mama says.

—

At night the fairy shrinks me. She shrinks me little so I can hold her hand, and we fly out the window. We fly way up into the night sky, going so fast the wind shouts in my ears. I'm higher than on the elephant, higher than on Ellis's shoulder. I'm so high I can see clear to River City, the place where Mama wants to live. The place that makes her smile. I can see it's flat, with a river winding through.

Then Jamie wakes me up. He drags his Indian blanket into my bed and shoves me over. He sticks his thumb in his mouth. He won't let go of the blanket even if Mama comes in and pulls.

Mama calls it a phase. She says Jamie is just upset because Daddy went away. She says we're all upset. But Mama has lost her mad face. She dresses in her fancy clothes for work, sparkly sweaters and tight skirts and rhinestones. She comes home so late Aunt Larue won't watch us and we have to stay at the neighbor lady's.

When Mama picks us up, me and Jamie are asleep. We walk across the wet grass with our eyes half-shut. Then Mama tells us a bedtime story. In the story Ellis took her dancing. "Tall men can really lead you," she says. "That's his height."

"Ellis can't dance as good as me," says Jamie.

"He has a boat," Mama says. "He dives under the ocean to look at whales and sharks."

This must be true because when Ellis picks Mama up for work his hair is slicked back nice like he just got out of the water. Then Mama comes out of the bedroom with her tight black skirt and tall high heels, her sweater with the sparkles falling down, and I have to hold my breath.

"Look at me!" Jamie calls when he sees Mama's eyes stuck on Ellis. And he dances hard like Fred Astaire. But Mama stands next to Ellis and says goodbye, and her head hides on his shoulder, like on the day we rode the elephant.

Jamie squeezes Mama's hand and tries to play with her gold bracelet, the tiny box with a key you can turn to play music. Mama squeezes back, then lets go. Her fingernails are new painted red and shiny; they smooth down her dress clear to her stockings with the seams up the back. Jamie has stopped dancing.

Silence

"Home from Reno," Ellis says when his movie projector is ready on Saturday night. He turns the knob and the film goes clickety and winds past the light. We eat popcorn sitting in the dark, and only the movie is bright. In the movie there is no sound, just silence. Ellis and Mama getting married in Reno.

Then they are home and bringing presents. There's a cowboy suit for Jamie and a cowgirl suit for me. I have a vest with fringe and a skirt with fringe and a hat with little dangling balls around the rim. Jamie has a vest and hat and two guns in holsters.

Now Ellis is our new daddy for sure. He's taller than our old daddy. His pipe smells sweet when he lights it. He throws me way high in the air and my stomach gets the red ribbons inside.

In the movie we're going out the front door, Mama first and Jamie next, doing his heel-toe across the lawn. I'm frozen on the porch with my face squinched up. The steps are so white they hurt my eyes.

"Do something," Mama's mouth says, "you're in the movies!" But I don't know what to do.

Jamie twirls over the lawn to the driveway. Even in the movie quiet I can hear his heel-toe's tapping noise. I can hear Mama clap her hands. She smiles, but Jamie doesn't.

Then the white spots start ballooning in the picture, which means the end. Jamie is running toward me through the white balloons. He holds up his gun. He points it at my chest. Bang, he says. You're dead.

The Promise

There's a noise in the dark, a big scary noise, *boom, boom, boom,* from the man with staring eyes and no hair and blotchy skin. My heart bangs like the bathroom pipes. I wake up and Mama's screaming. She runs into our room and tells Jamie to hurry into my bed. The big noise that was in my sleep is still going on outside it. *Boom. Boom. Boom.*

"Why?" Jamie says. Now that New Daddy lives here, Jamie isn't supposed to get in bed with me.

"Just do it!" says Mama.

"Is it Daddy?"

"Hush." Mama isn't screaming now. She's whispering. Jamie flicks the switch and the yellow light bursts out before she turns it off again. "Don't turn on the light," she says.

My eyes keep the yellow spots even when the light goes off. I try to see with just the clown-face night-light. The noise goes on, and me and Mama and Jamie listen into it. *Boom. Boom. Boom. Boom.*

"Somebody's breaking down our door." Jamie wraps his Indian blanket over me. It's hot under the blanket, a crawly hot like bugs are in here.

"Damn it," Mama cusses. "Where are the police?"

"He's getting in!" yells Jamie.

"Ellis won't let him." Mama's arms go hard around us, rocking. I'm squished up next to Jamie until I can hardly breathe. Then there's a different sound from all the rest. The air goes *crack*. Mama jumps when she hears it.

"I bet that was a gun!" says Jamie.

"You kids stay here." Mama opens the door. New Daddy and Old Daddy are in the light. Mama hurries out and the door slams shut.

The clown-face night-light goes out. Jamie throws off his Indian blanket, and we both jump up and bump the wall. I don't want to stay in here. Those crawly bugs are everywhere. When Jamie finds the door he opens it and we run out quick. New Daddy is holding Old Daddy in his arms like they're hugging, but they're not hugging. Then Old Daddy says, "Umph!"

Jamie is right. I see a gun on the floor. Not like Jamie's cowboy gun but more important.

"Don't touch that!" Mama yells. "Get back!"

"I'll kill you!" Old Daddy shouts. "You'll never take my kids away. I'll kill you first!"

"Don't kill him, Daddy!" I say. "That's our new daddy!"

Old Daddy hears me. He goes crumpled and starts to cry.

"He's drunk," Mama says. "He doesn't mean it." She pushes us back in our room and shuts the door again.

Me and Jamie hold hands in the crawly dark. I don't know if Old Daddy has killed New Daddy or not. I hear other sounds, like people running inside, and more voices. Some are squawky and some are deep.

"We've got him," the deep voice says. I can hear the squawky voice talking at the same time. Jamie opens the door. Two big policemen are in our house. One of them holds a box the squawky voice comes from. The other one stares at the place where our front door used to be. He crosses Old Daddy's arms behind his back.

Old Daddy is still crying. He's sad because New Daddy took us away. I get a hole in my chest and my stomach squeezes. Jamie runs and hugs him, and then I do, too.

"Promise me you won't forget your daddy?" Old Daddy cries. "Promise to love me best, forever?"

I look at New Daddy, who isn't dead, but standing right by Mama.

"I promise!" I say, "I promise," right after Jamie does.

The Lucky Place

I try to keep my promise, but it's hard. After the police take Old Daddy away, we never see him. Jamie says it's because he's locked in jail, but Mama says that's nonsense, he's welcome to visit us anytime he wants. He'll be back, Mama says. But how will he know where to look? We aren't staying in our brown-grass house. New Daddy sold his boat to buy us a new house on Diamond Street.

Diamond Street doesn't have diamonds on it but is paved

like all the other roads in River City. And there really is a river, only it's too far away to see. Jamie says the houses go in threes, which means every time you count to three, the next house will be the same as the first one. Except for the house on the corner, which is two-story and looks like the ones on the other corners.

On moving day, when I see the two-story house on the corner of Diamond Street, I hope New Daddy will stop there, but he doesn't. He keeps driving past it and down the hill to the bottom. The trailer full of our furniture and toys clacks and creaks behind us, and Mama turns around looking worried.

"It's nothing," New Daddy says. Jamie is counting the houses and New Daddy stops when he says three.

"Do we have a chimney?" Jamie begs when we get out. "I want a chimney."

"It's just built," says Mama. "And it's got a picture window. Look."

A picture window is a big lot of glass that shows from the front yard. In the front yard there's a little tree tied up with two sticks and yellow string. The grass in our front yard is Easter green and runs right into the Easter green grass in the neighbor's yard, so it's almost like having two yards. All the back-yards run together, too.

"There's lots of kids to play with," Mama says. "And they're going to put in that freeway and the shopping center right down the road." She says the white horse that runs in the field where the shopping center will be means good luck, that we have moved to a lucky place. She licks her thumb and stamps it into her palm to seal it. Then New Daddy laughs and grabs her stamped hand and Mama's cheeks get pink.

She waves to a woman across the street, who stands outside a number-three house like ours. Mama says the woman's name is Janet Candy.

"Her kids are about the same age as you." Mama watches New Daddy put the key in the lock. "But you're not to go across the street without holding hands. Ellis?"

New Daddy has picked Mama up like a baby. She has to hug his neck.

"Your mama's going to quit the El Rancho," New Daddy says to us, "and stay here with you kids." He carries her inside. He twirls her around. When he sets her down, they kiss. I close my eyes, but the sound is everywhere in the empty room. When I open my eyes there's lots of light from the picture window. The walls are bright and the wood floor golden. The front door feels too heavy to break.

Mama's right. This is a lucky, lucky place.

Jamie takes my hand. He's happy, too. We run across the floor and our shoes pound loud. We find a kitchen and a dining room, with a real glass door to the backyard. We find a bedroom and a bathroom on one side of the house, and three bedrooms and a bathroom on the other.

The bedrooms smell brand-new.

"This one is mine," Jamie says about the big one.

But Mama comes in and says, "Nothing doing. This bedroom is for Ellis and me." She says Jamie will have the room with the high window that looks at the backyard. And I get a room all my own, too, the little one up front.

I jump up happy but Jamie fusses. "I don't like that room," he says and my feet go still. "I want the one on the other side of the house."

Mama puts her finger to her lips. She looks down the hall to see if New Daddy's coming to find us. "That room is for company," she says.

"Like who?" says Jamie.

"Like Ellis's mother, for instance. Your new grandma."

"But she won't be here all the time."

"And Ellis's children, have you forgotten about them?"

Jamie folds up his arms. His mouth goes twisty. "I could give it back when they come."

But Mama wants him close. "That's clear across the house," she says.

"I *want* to be across the house." Jamie gets his whiny voice.

"Hush," says Mama, because we hear New Daddy's footsteps. My stomach squeezes. Jamie never knows how to be extra good.

"You can have my room," I say, even though I don't want to say it.

"I don't want your stupid room!" Jamie yells at me.

New Daddy comes in. His voice is like he's making a joke, but it's not a joke, too. "Don't talk to your sister that way," he says, "unless you want a knuckle sandwich."

Coral Reef

New Daddy has a new job. He is going to drive a truck full of ice cream, milk, and eggs. He takes us all to a grown-up place called the Coral Reef to celebrate. Inside is dark, with giant nets on the ceilings and seashells in the nets. There are fish tanks bubbling in the walls and candles on every table. We're all dressed up like for church. Mama told me to wear my blue scratchy dress, but it's too tight around the arms. "I just bought that," is what she says, but she lets me wear the red one instead.

Mama doesn't like red—red is not a good color for redheads. But I'm not a redhead. "What am I, Mama?" I say at the Coral Reef.

"You have black hair like Daddy," Jamie says. He keeps kicking his chair leg. Mama twists her rhinestone necklace. She orders a grown-up drink. She's wearing her lilac dress, which she bought to get married in Reno. She keeps her hand on New Daddy's hand and her fingers curl up under his shirtsleeve. I tell Jamie that New Daddy has black hair, too, even if it isn't curly.

"But you didn't get your hair from him," Jamie says.

New Daddy winks at me, and my stomach gets a tiny red ribbon. He lifts Mama's hand and kisses her wrist, and Jamie gets up to look at the fish.

"You won't always be a Milk Maid man," says Mama. "They'll see how smart you are and put you in the office."

"Maybe," New Daddy says. "But I'm happy driving the truck for now." He waves at Jamie. "Come on back so we can order."

"I want steak, can I have steak?" Jamie begs when he comes back.

"Shhh." Mama smiles at New Daddy. "That's too expensive. You and Cass can share the chicken."

Jamie shakes his head. "I hate chicken."

"Since when?" Mama makes her warning lips.

"Jamie," says New Daddy, "I'm going to have a big truck to drive for Milk Maid. What do you think, want to go along in the morning to pick her up?"

"I want to go!" I say when Jamie doesn't answer.

"Hush, Cass," Mama says. "It's for boys. And Jamie wants to go."

After dinner Mama orders one more grown-up drink, to have while New Daddy smokes his pipe. When New Daddy lights the pipe his cheeks go in and the smoke comes out. He touches Mama's hair and puffs. The sweet smoke makes me sleepy.

"Must be time to go," New Daddy says, and I open my eyes. I didn't even know they were shut.

But Mama says the band is setting up. "Just one dance, honey, what do you say?"

"I have to get up in the morning. And the kids look beat."

"Oh, come on. They won't mind. You won't mind, will you?" Mama asks Jamie and me.

"I'll dance with you, Mama," Jamie says.

"Any other takers?" Mama looks at New Daddy. She tugs on his arm. Music goes tinkly through the Coral Reef and Mama's laugh is tinkly, too.

New Daddy smiles and puts down his pipe. "You first, Snikelfritz," he says. He's talking to me.

"But I can't dance with pigeon toes," I say.

"Wanna bet?" New Daddy says. "Watch." He swings me up and I sail out. I land with my feet on top of his feet, and my hands inside his hands. Then when he dances I'm dancing, too. I feel big on top of his shoes, even if my arms can hardly reach.

"Jamie?" says New Daddy when we stop. "You want a turn?"

Jamie kicks his chair leg. He says he already knows how to dance. So New Daddy sails me back into my chair and takes

Mama's hand. Then he wraps his arms around her, and Mama squishes up close and whispers in his ear.

"Oh, brother." Jamie kicks and kicks his chair. "I can dance better than that," he says. I wish he'd stop. I sit perfectly still. I like watching Mama and New Daddy. They are pretty as the king and queen in our storybook. And when they turn in circles, the candlelight bursts on Mama's necklace and the rhinestones sparkle like baby stars.

In the Dark

"The reason Daddy won't come back," Jamie whispers to me in the dark, "is because of *him*." He's got his Indian blanket under the covers with us. He isn't supposed to be here. On Diamond Street, Mama gets really mad if she catches him. She says, what would Ellis think of a big boy like him in bed with his sister? But I don't tell. I don't like Jamie being scared.

"Mama says he's our daddy now," I say.

"He's not our daddy. Daddy is our daddy." Jamie rubs and rubs his Indian blanket.

"Don't you want to ride in his big truck? And Mama said he's going to make us a real train for Christmas."

"I don't want any train." Jamie pinches my arm. "Wouldn't you rather have Daddy back?"

"I don't know. What does he look like?"

"You don't even remember your own daddy? Jeez, you're dumb."

"I am not. I can too remember." But when I close my eyes and try to see him, I just see New Daddy's face instead.

"Ellis is mean. He's always telling me what to do." Jamie's voice is plugged up around his thumb. "I'm not going to call him Daddy. I'm not even going to talk to him."

"He kisses Mama a lot."

"It's no big deal. Anybody can kiss."

I turn away from him. I feel hot, then I feel cold. Jamie forgot to shut my door and the hall light shines in my eyes.

Mama says we have to have the hall light for when she gets up to check on us. I hope she's already checked tonight. Jamie won't go back in his bed. His head scrunches my arm. He kicks me in his sleep.

Neapolitan

"Jamie, Jamie." Mama shakes us. She pulls Jamie out of bed and takes his Indian blanket away. "Remember you're supposed to ride in the truck this morning? Shhh," she says when Jamie whines. "Of course you want to go."

"No, I don't. I want to sleep."

"Don't be silly. It's a big truck. You'll sit up high."

I rub my eyes. Jamie tries to get back in bed with me, but Mama won't let him.

"You're not sleeping in here," she says. "What have I told you?"

"I was scared."

"Okay, but it's morning now. Go on in the bathroom and get dressed."

Mama pulls Jamie by the arm. "I'll go," I say, but she isn't listening to me.

"Too early for him?" I hear New Daddy in the hall. "That's okay, don't make him."

But Mama says Jamie will wake up once he's dressed.

"Oh, God, keep your fingers crossed," Mama says. New Daddy and Jamie are coming home in the Milk Maid truck together. Mama hopes they had fun. "They are going to be pals," she says, "you'll see."

I want to be pals, too, but Mama says Ellis has Jamie and she has me. She's making us look-alike dresses. I have to stand still when she pins the pattern on me or I get poked. When I say I don't want look-alike dresses Mama says, "Of course you do, you'll be so cute." But I won't look pretty like her. "Why are you so stubborn?" she says. She turns me around. The pattern paper crinkles and her pointy nails dig the pins out. "Slip it off, let's go see."

I love the Milk Maid truck. It roars up giant in the driveway. It's painted milk white and there's a girl on one side who looks exactly like the girl on the other side. She's wearing a red-checked apron and her hair is in braids. Her hand holds a milk bottle up and she looks so happy about it.

"I'm glad it's only temporary," Mama says about the truck. "He won't be driving that thing for long." It sounds like thunder until New Daddy shuts it off. Then it screeches and shakes and goes still. New Daddy jumps out one side and Jamie jumps out the other.

"Well?" Mama says when Jamie won't say anything. "How was it?"

"He did fine." New Daddy pats Jamie's shoulder, and that makes Mama happy. But Jamie moves until New Daddy isn't touching him anymore.

"I got ice cream," Jamie tells me. "It's called Neapolitan." He has a whole carton. He shows me the picture on the side, of vanilla, chocolate, and strawberry.

"I'm going to ride in the truck next time," I whisper to him.

"Who cares?" says Jamie, loud.

He runs into the house and Mama says to New Daddy, "I bet he had fun."

"Well, you know," New Daddy says, "he's not really crazy about trucks."

Top Drawer

The things New Daddy likes to do are in the garage. He has a baseball and a football and a hockey stick. He has hammers and saws and nails. When I come out to watch he uses his biggest saw and cuts some boards and the sawdust flies.

"Where's Jamie?" he asks me. "Does he want to help?"

"I'll help," I say, but New Daddy makes a creasy face.

"In that dress? Your mother'd skin me alive."

I look down at my dress and start to hate it. "Is that the Christmas train?" I say. "For me and Jamie?"

"For all of you kids." He grabs my nose and squeezes. When he pulls his hand away my nose is stuck in his fingers. "Got your nose," he says, and laughs. "Now where's your brother?"

But Jamie doesn't want to help. He wants to play with me instead. On Diamond Street, Mama doesn't care if we go in the front yard alone. We can water the little tree down by the street and we can run around and around the house through the grass. We play the Bible stories Jamie knows, about Roman emperors and slave girls, about the horrible curses like locusts and floods that God puts on bad people. Then we play a game from our new TV.

It's the end of the world and there's hot lava everywhere. People go around killing other people and you can't step in the lava and you have to run from the bad guys, who are ugly with mushroom faces from the atomic bomb blasts. The swing set that New Daddy stuck in the ground is safe. If you're on the swing set the mushroom people can't get you.

"Come on," Jamie says when we escape. "Follow me."

In Mama and New Daddy's room, the shades are pulled down tight. It's cool and smells like her perfume. Her drawers have everything we're not allowed to touch. Jamie opens them and we stick our hands in and there are so many layers, deep with ribbon and lace. When Mama wears these things they slither and whisper, and New Daddy kisses her so big I have to close my eyes extra hard.

Jamie pulls out a black thing. He steps his legs into the black thing's legs and yanks it over his pants. The black thing hangs on Jamie and gives him a pointy chest.

"Don't tell," he says, so I promise not to. I would never tell on Jamie.

He finds Mama's nightie, the short gray one with ruffles, and slides it over my head. He spins me around until the ruffles float out. Then he uses Mama's red lipstick. He draws it around his mouth like a clown's. "Hold still," he says, and gives me a clown mouth, too.

"Watch out the window," Jamie says. He uses the black pencil to paint lines around his eyes. He colors his cheeks with powder. I lift the shade and look at Mama, who's gone into the front yard to work. She's planting flowers around the little tree. The little tree is leaning over, so she stops and ties its yellow string tighter.

"Oh, dawwwling," Jamie calls, jumping on the bed. He stretches out his hands and marches back and forth. He dances his heel-toe. "Come on, I'll teach you," he says. I jump on the bed and we hold hands. "Dawwwling, dawwwling," we say and bounce.

The garage door bangs and Jamie freezes. He tries to pull the black thing off, only it's too late. New Daddy is coming down the hall. He opens the bedroom door. From the way he looks, I think he might give Jamie a knuckle sandwich now.

School

I jump off the porch and run after Jamie down Diamond Street. "Go back," Jamie says. "You can't come."

Jamie has to go to school. Mama says school will be good for him, with all those other little boys to play with. I don't want Jamie to play with other little boys. I want him to play with me. "Why can't I go?" I beg. "I got in Mama's drawers, too."

"Babies don't go to school," Jamie says. But he's only mad at me because he can't stay home. I stomp back and sit on the porch and watch him get smaller and smaller until finally he's a tiny dot that turns the corner. My stomach squeezes. Next year I'll go to school, and then I'll play with Jamie all the time.

Our neighbor Janet Candy comes across the street. She and Mama sit on the high stools by the kitchen to have a beer. They talk talk talk. Janet talks smoky. She knows everything about the people on Diamond Street, and she tells Mama everything she knows. "Jesus H. Christ," she says, "son of a bitch." She slaps the counter and cigarette smoke rushes out her nose.

I can listen if I pretend not to, and play with the Lincoln Logs quiet on the floor. There are people called Catholics who keep having kids and people called stuck-up who have too much money, and there's even a crazy lady who lives next door. "Crazee," says Janet Candy. "She won't come out of her house, not even for her boys."

Mama is not worried about the Catholics or the crazy lady. She tells Janet Candy that she always wanted to live in River City. She says it's nothing like our old neighborhood, believe you me. Then she has to tell Janet Candy about Old Daddy because Jamie has already spilled the beans. That's what Janet Candy says, your kid spilled the beans. So Mama tells Janet Candy lots of things that I've never heard before. Like how much New Daddy misses his own little boy and girl. And how we're going to see them for Christmas, if he can get them away from that witch. Mama says he'd get them more if the witch would let him. I'm sure New Daddy will get his children away from the witch. He's so strong he can do anything.

Jamie walks faster coming home from school. He's got his hands full of papers with drawings on them and he runs toward me when he sees me, making the drawings flutter like wings. He doesn't want to help New Daddy in the garage with the Christmas train, and he doesn't want to ride in the Milk Maid truck. I'm glad because that means he'll play with me.

We go into Mama's closet and find her oldest skirts. Jamie begs Mama to let us wear them until Mama says okay. But I have to be the girl, Mama says, and Jamie has to wear his skirt for a cape, like Superman or Zorro. We go outside in the back-yard and Jamie waits until Mama isn't watching so he can put on her skirt like a skirt. This time when he runs from the hot lava he's too slow, and the hot lava melts his feet.

"I'm a gypsy!" he screams. "Help me or else!" And I have to try and throw him a rope from the swing, but the rope is too short and Jamie keeps melting.

"Grab it, Jamie!" I say, but he won't.

"A pox on you!" he cries. "And on all your children!" And he turns and twists on the lawn, taking a long time getting dead.

Lightning

Mama wakes me up when the lightning jumps. Wind knocks the little tree outside the house. Rain hits hard against the roof. I'm afraid to get out of bed. "Come on," she says, "it's your daddy." I don't know what she means.

The floor is cold. I can see the big dark at the door of my room, with the thin light behind. Without light the hallway looks like a tunnel. He's at the other end. Then he's coming down the tunnel, and the lightning cracks. He swoops me up and I smell the rain and his wet coat and funny breath. "Kiss," he says.

I'm on his knee. His arm sticks me close. Now I remember how Old Daddy's eyes are very blue, and his hair is curly black. I remember the picture in the yard at the brown-grass house, how Old Daddy tried to hold me and Jamie but couldn't. And he brought our cheeks right up smash against his cheeks like he'd never let us go.

Old Daddy still hugs like he'll never let go. He still wears the big gold ring. He pulls me into the living room where the lights are. He looks at New Daddy standing there; then he takes something from his pocket.

Money. Lots of dollars wound up, with a gold pin to keep them in place. Old Daddy opens the roll and the money flaps down. He licks his thumb so his thumb can count. One, two. He sets them on the table. The way he looks at New Daddy I think he's giving them to him, but he isn't, he's giving them to Jamie and me.

"A Jackson each," he says. "You two being good?" Old Daddy moves like a haywire toy. He bumps against a chair.

"What about the boat? Are we going to the river?" Jamie wants to know.

Mama looks worried at Old Daddy. I can't tell what this means. I hope she won't make me go on any boat with him tonight. But I might have to go to keep the money.

"It's raining." Mama takes New Daddy's hand. Old Daddy looks at Mama and his face goes flat, like somebody stepped on it.

"And your old man's under the weather," Old Daddy says.

"But you promised!" Jamie cries.

"So sad, too bad, your dad." Old Daddy bumps his way to the door. Jamie runs in front of him. My heart goes thud because Jamie is crying. Old Daddy looks at him and everything stops. Then he opens the door and the wind blows in. He puts his hand on Jamie's head.

The door slaps shut. Jamie runs to the window and jerks open the drapes. Old Daddy's headlights show the rain. The rain is like a thousand needles coming down. The headlights sit still for a while; then they get big in the glass until Jamie and the window are all lit up. "He'll be back," Mama tells Jamie, and the light slides out of the window.

Spotlight

Mama and New Daddy buy Jamie dancing lessons to cheer him up. The teacher's name is Reece. Reece dances so good he's been on TV. "One together, two, one together, two," he says, and smiles like he's everybody's friend. Then he goes leaping through the room full of mirrors in his tight black pants and shirt.

Mama says Jamie is the best boy in the class, even though he's the only boy in class, except for Reece's son. She sews him a tall white soldier hat and shiny blue soldier pants so he can dance the Little Toy Soldier on stage. The soldier pants need a soldier jacket, and Mama sews that too. She stitches gold stripes called braid all the way down both arms.

Backstage smells like dust and lots of people crowded together. The girls from Jamie's dance class are dressed like my ballerina doll. They wear spangly tutus with sequins down the front. They whisper and giggle and shove, and one girl starts to cry.

Jamie is too brave to cry. He's got on the soldier jacket and his eyes are extra blue and his cheeks are extra pink. He's counting to himself like he already hears the music, and when the curtains fly open he'll be in front of all the people, but I'll still be hidden under the wings. I think of everybody watching Jamie and my stomach squeezes, and I have to hold my breath so he won't make any mistakes.

People clap clap clap when the curtain cord screeches and they see Jamie standing there with his knee lifted up. Reece is behind the curtain, but I can still see him hiding. He sets the phonograph needle down. It sounds scratchy until Jamie's music starts. Jamie keeps his hands out like he's walking a tightrope, but he isn't going to fall. His right foot taps him across the stage so fast you can hardly see it, then his left foot taps him back again.

The lights are off, except for the round, fat light on Jamie. That's a spotlight, like the one that lights up the sky for sales at the grocery store. And when Jamie is in the spotlight, he's the one who shines.

Afterward he runs backstage and Mama and New Daddy hurry to see him.

"That was perfect," Mama says. "Just perfect!"

And New Daddy's eyes have the little happy lights in them. "Wow," he says. "You were really, really good."

That makes Jamie smile so big his mouth must hurt. Right away I decide I'm going to dance, too, when I get rid of these stupid pigeon toes.

Jacksons

Me and Jamie are playing catch with New Daddy when Old Daddy comes back. I feel sorry that we can't play anymore, but Jamie drops the ball and runs.

Old Daddy gets out of his car and New Daddy holds out his hand, but Old Daddy won't shake it. Mama comes outside with her too-good smile. Old Daddy bends down laughing and hugs me like he'll never let go. I'm afraid when he does this because New Daddy is watching. What if he thinks I like Old Daddy better? But I'm supposed to like Old Daddy better, is what Jamie says, and anyway I promised.

We go in the house and Old Daddy pulls out his gold money clip. He unfolds the bills. He wets his thumb on his tongue and the money flaps down.

"Two Jacksons," he says, and slides them out and sets them curved up on the kitchen counter. This time I know the Jacksons are for Jamie and me, but we have to wait until he tells us they're ours.

We're going home with Old Daddy today and we'll ride in the boat tomorrow. Mama says we can take the money with us, so I run to get my green velvet purse. The purse is round like a hat with tiny pearls sewn around the rim. It closes with a cord.

"You know about boats, don't you?" Mama follows me into my room. "You can't get near the edge. You can't climb around on top. Stay right with Jamie," Mama says.

I hide my Jackson in my purse. The Jackson has a man on it with a funny head. He looks up at me.

"You have to wear a life jacket," Mama says.

"What's that?"

Mama looks worried at me like I'm going to cross the street alone. She chews her lip. "Do you remember what happened at the races?"

I feel funny when she says this. Like she wants me to go and not to go. But Old Daddy has already given me the Jackson. I don't say anything.

"No, you were too little," Mama says. "And anyway, Sikes is sober today. Just keep the yellow hat on. And stay with Jamie."

The yellow hat is itchy and ties under my chin. "I don't like it," I say.

"Of course you do," Mama says, like she always does about the stuff she makes me wear. Then we go find Old Daddy.

Old Daddy grabs my hand and Mama's nails are sharp in my shoulder. She hugs me hard, and Jamie, too. "Watch your sister," she tells Jamie. "Don't forget to call."

"I won't."

"I'm counting on you. Make sure she wears the yellow hat, and keep her away from the edge."

"I will."

New Daddy taps her shoulder and Mama stands up and stops hugging us. I kiss New Daddy quick and then Jamie is pulling on our hands, heading us for the door. "The hat!" Mama says another time. "Don't forget!"

A Baby

Old Daddy drives us downtown. It takes a long time and is way past the river. Jamie sits up front so he can see how they're building the new freeway today. I sit in back, where I can't see much except the phone poles skipping by, pulled by the drooping wires. Right away Old Daddy starts telling me I shouldn't kiss New Daddy. I feel strange when he says this, like I did something wrong I'm in trouble for. *I told you so*, goes Jamie's face when he looks over the seat at me. I open my velvet purse and feel my Jackson. It smells old, and it feels like the sandpaper New Daddy uses in the garage when it's almost worn away.

"So your mother's going to have another one, huh?" Old Daddy says to Jamie. "That didn't take them long."

When we're with Old Daddy, I try to forget New Daddy and Mama, and to love him best like I promised I would. I try to imagine staying with him forever, which Jamie says he wishes we could do.

Old Daddy's place is not like our lucky place on Diamond Street. He lives in one room, which has pretty wood furniture in it but no pictures on the walls. You have to use the bathroom down the hall that other people use. On the floor is a gray rug where the flowers are rubbed out from people's footsteps. And the room smells funny, like something too sweet. I wonder if this is Old Daddy's house, but he says it's just a rented room, with rented furniture, which I don't understand. If you live someplace, wouldn't the furniture belong to you?

But only the things on the dresser belong to Old Daddy. The dresser has a white cloth hanging down, with a mirror above it that comes from a cord nailed to the wall. The mirror tilts so I can see Old Daddy's things. His cigarettes are squished and wrinkled in the ashtray. There are coins from his pocket, and his cuff links. The cuff links seem like buttons with little noses out the back. I wish I could have one, but I'm afraid to ask. Next to the cuff links is Old Daddy's hat and a bottle with a scrolly picture.

"Having another one" means Mama is getting a baby. Old Daddy keeps asking us lots of questions about Mama, which Jamie tries to answer. Then it's time to go to dinner. Old Daddy says you have to look nice for the 21 Club, but he can't do my hair. He pulls it and makes it hurt underneath. He calls me Baby Doll and Jamie is his Little Man. He says we are the smartest, most handsome children in the whole world. He sets his hat on his head. "Give your old daddy a hug," he says, and mashes us close.

Then he opens his lighter to have a Chesterfield and the flame pops up. He laughs and pushes his hat back, and his eyes crinkle shut, his mouth draws in, like what happens to my purse when I pull the cord. His face stays this way and he looks all around, still laughing. I laugh too when he pokes me, but then I feel strange. Nothing seems funny. It's harder than I thought to love Old Daddy.

"That's it, Baby Doll," Old Daddy says, pulling his hat back down. "Laugh and the world laughs with you, weep and you weep alone. Does your mother still say that one?"

"All the time," Jamie says.

The Boat

In the morning Old Daddy takes us on the boat, which belongs to his brother, Uncle Del. Jamie reminds him about the yellow hat just when I thought he'd forgotten. I've never been on a boat before. It goes fast down the river. It's loud and the front plops up and down and makes the water fan. The top of my hat sails up and down too. The trees on the bank look thirsty and rush backwards. Behind me Old Daddy holds Jamie on his lap, and Jamie looks so happy. I wish I could be happy. I watch Uncle Del, who has curly hair like Old Daddy's but eyes that aren't nearly as blue.

I don't want the boat to stop. I like getting wet from the

parted, brown river water. A big bird with droopy wings races us. Then Uncle Del stops the boat and only my ears are rushing.

Uncle Del sits in a chair next to Old Daddy, holding two glasses with ice.

"You kids want a Coke?" Old Daddy says. But we haven't even had breakfast yet. Jamie nods and Old Daddy pops off the lid and hands me a whole one to myself. "You need a glass?" Old Daddy asks. I shake my head. I tell him how New Daddy had a boat too, but he sold it to get us our lucky house in River City. Old Daddy looks at me sharp and his smile goes away.

"Who you calling Daddy? I'm your daddy."

I hold my Coke bottle tight. A boat goes slapping by and we bounce up and then down.

"Mama says we have to call him that," says Jamie. "But I don't call him anything." Which is a lie—Jamie calls him Daddy too, sometimes.

"Well, I'm your daddy," Old Daddy says again. "Comeer." And he grabs me and sticks me on his knee. "Who's your daddy, Baby Doll?"

"You are," I say. I hug his neck. His skin smells salty by his shirt. The strangeness comes up in my stomach like a snake.

"Don't let them tell you any different. We'd still be together if not for him." He pours grown-up drink into the glasses of ice Uncle Del is holding. He drinks his down.

"Relax, Sikes," says Uncle Del.

Old Daddy pours more drink. "Del and me didn't have a pot to piss in when we grew up," he says. "No sir. When Mama died our daddy sent us to the orphans' home. Can you imagine that? I got whipped so much I ran away. Ran away home and

Daddy put me to work. Drove the backwoods in a bootleg car. No wonder I learned to drink. But I sold papers. I shined shoes. I was a soda jerk and then I went into the mines. I even helped build the great Hoover Dam. You kids can be proud of your old man for that. You can always be proud. What the hell is some cook compared to that?"

"He's not a cook now," I say. "He drives the Milk Maid truck." Old Daddy looks mad at me and I climb off his lap.

"Let's fish," says Uncle Del.

"Angel Merit was buried alive in the Hoover Dam," Old Daddy says. "They were pouring and he fell. Nothing anybody could do. Just like that. Solid concrete over his head."

"Never mind," says Uncle Del. He tells me and Jamie to sit holding the poles. Old Daddy doesn't look at me. He keeps telling us about his Angel friend, all twisted up and buried in concrete. When our arms get tired Uncle Del sticks the poles in holders and says to watch the lines.

It's hot. A mosquito gets stuck under my hat. It whines and bites my forehead. I pull the hat off, but Old Daddy still isn't looking. He's in his chair with his hat down low, drinking more grown-up drink.

Jamie and I eat crackers and cheese. We watch the lines. The boat is still until another boat comes by, when it heaves and bounces. Jamie sits by Old Daddy, but I stand at the rail. I feel sorry for Old Daddy, for being an orphan and having to work so hard, and sorry I made him mad. I'm going to try harder to love him. I don't want to think about home, but then I do, and my stomach goes up and doesn't come down. Old Daddy and Uncle Del are raising their glasses, raising and lowering, laughing.

21 Club

When we get back to the hotel Old Daddy says he has to go out for a while. He tells us to lay down in the bed and go to sleep. "How about giving your old man his Jacksons back?" he says.

Jamie digs in his pocket. He gives Old Daddy his Jackson. "Cassie?" Old Daddy asks. "What do you say? Come on, Baby Doll, your old man is broke." He has his floppy smile.

I shake my head. I don't want to give Old Daddy back his Jackson. "Where are you going?" I say when my stomach squeezes.

"Out for a nightcap," Old Daddy says.

I shake my head again. I squish my green velvet purse. "Just wear the hat you have on," I beg.

"Jesus, Mary, and Joseph." Old Daddy laughs until his eyes get leaky. "Just wear the hat you have on!" Then he walks out the door like the haywire toy.

Jamie yells at me. "Why didn't you give him his money? What's the matter with you?"

"He said it was mine," I yell back, even though I don't want to yell. Even though I don't want Jamie to be mad at me.

Jamie won't talk to me now. He goes to the window and looks out. I sit on the bed. There's nothing to do, so I play with the coins on the dresser. There are dimes and nickels and pennies. I stack them up and push them over. Stack them up and push them over. My hands shake. My face is tingly hot.

Old Daddy takes forever. He comes back smiling. He wants the Jackson again but I won't give it. "No!" I say when Jamie tries to grab my purse.

"Never mind," Old Daddy tells him. "You kids come with me."

We go back to the 21 Club, and sit in a cabinet without doors. There's lots of cabinets in the 21 Club, with tables and wooden benches inside. Old Daddy gives us quarters and we pick out music from the fat machine with lights in its belly. Then he tells us to stay put while he sees his friend at the bar. Jamie is still mad at me, so I watch Old Daddy in the mirror with the hundred glass bottles. I can see him when he pushes his hat back to laugh.

Old Daddy comes back from the bar. "Want to dance for a drink?" he asks Jamie. "Ned over there doesn't believe that you can tap. Get up on the bar and he'll give us a round."

Jamie makes a monkey face at me. "I can do it easy," he says. He jumps up and takes Old Daddy's hand.

"Don't move from this spot, Baby Doll." When Old Daddy hugs me I hear his puffy breath, and I feel strange again, like on the boat, like he knows I can't help but love New Daddy more.

Everybody claps when Jamie dances. His feet make the bar top sing. He watches me and then he forgets to watch me anymore. But I have to keep my eyes right on him. I press my head against the bench. Jamie will dance forever. I try not to shut my eyes. The music is loud and then it's far away. It's like I'm on the boat again the way the room bounces up and the bottles wave on the shelves.

In the Box

I don't know where I am. I'm in a box and the box sides are pushing me. My head is at the bottom. I open my eyes and the box is just the bench in the 21 Club. My head is on the seat. The noise is gone. Jamie, Old Daddy, and Old Daddy's friends are gone. A lady is shaking me.

"Hal, look here. He left her," the lady says. And the bartender says, "That damn Sikes."

"Where's your daddy, little girl?" the lady says. She has green paint on top of her eyes. I've never seen green paint like that before. I sit up straight. My stomach squeezes so hard it wants to be sick.

"You'd better take her home with you," the bartender says.

"Christ." The lady looks at the ceiling, then at me.

"Well, come on, kid. We're closing. Look, don't be stubborn, you can't stay here."

I can't breathe. I don't know what to do. After a long time, I stand up.

Outside is dark and cold. The lady holds my hand. Her heels go click on the sidewalk. She walks so fast I have to run to keep up. The streets are scary dark. A car light pushes my eyes. The lady's hand is cold and bigger than Mama's hand. Mama is going to be mad. She says never ever talk to strangers. But Mama isn't here. I get floaty like a balloon, and like myself watching the balloon, going smaller and smaller in the sky.

Wall Bed

"My name is Geraldine," the lady says. "Sit here." We had to climb stairs to get to her house; my legs wobble at the top. I sit down and a bunch of dolls are staring at me. I squeeze my eyes and the dolls are still there, all lined up on a shelf. They have real hair and wear tiny grown-up clothes. Blue and orange and pink ruffled dresses with matching coats and hats. Their cheeks are as red as apples and they have real stockings and high-heeled shoes on their feet. Geraldine keeps talking.

"Don't touch," she says. "Those are storybook dolls and they're expensive." But I wouldn't touch her storybook dolls. "Look at that sunburn," she says. "We'd better put some vinegar on that. I'm going to make me some scrambled eggs. Would you like that, little girl?"

I want to tell her my name's Cassie and I'm not hungry, but she's already in the kitchen cracking eggs. I try and touch the tips of all my fingers together, like in church, only my fingers won't hold still. I make my shaky fingers go inside my hands so I can talk to them. "Here's the church," I say, "here's the steeple. Open the door and see all the people." But when I open my hands, there's really nobody there.

Geraldine comes out with a skinny-necked bottle full of red stuff. "This will cool you down," she says and pats the red stuff on my face. It's so smelly my eyes sting. I put my church hands down between my knees. The storybook dolls are watching me.

"Don't you cry," says Geraldine. "I left him a note. Your daddy will come find you when he sobers up. Let's go eat our eggs."

I don't want to move. I want to stay by the door, and listen good in case Old Daddy has already sobered up and is coming back to find me.

"Little girl." Geraldine makes skinny eyes at me. "We are not going to waste those eggs!"

In the kitchen, the eggs steam on the plate. I slide my fork in careful so I won't spill. I try to eat her eggs. I worry Old Daddy might come and I can't hear the stairs from here. I promise myself if he comes now, I'll love him forever and ever, even better than I love New Daddy.

I'm not a balloon anymore, I'm not floating away. But Geraldine keeps changing places. First she's sitting beside me and then she's standing up. She's eating and then she's eaten every speck of egg. She's got lots of money in her droopy apron pockets, the apron she wore at the 21 Club. She's got wavy stacks of nickels and dimes and quarters, and a pile of dollar bills. "Tip money," she says. "Don't touch."

She tells me to close my eyes and not to peek. I close my eyes and they feel scratchy inside. Geraldine gets up from the table and is gone a long time. I crack open my eyes and she's holding a storybook doll. She unsnaps the doll's orange ruffled dress and hides some dollar bills inside. Then she snaps the dress shut.

"Little girl," she says, "I'll sing you a German song. Come out here."

Geraldine brushes my hair while she sings. German is spooky and doesn't have any words I know, and the brush yanks. "You don't talk, do you?" Her face is big, looking around my shoulder. "I like that. I'd like a little girl who didn't talk. Who sat so quiet and ate her food. I should keep you myself, eh?" There's a brown dot on her chin with hairs growing out of it. The green paint is fuzzy on her eyes.

I make my hands go way down inside my knees and press.

Geraldine stands up. She pulls on a wall and the wall starts to fall. She doesn't try to stop it. The wall falls to the floor and a bed is there, *poof*, like magic. Geraldine tugs on the sheets. She sticks her hand under the pillow.

"You can wear this," she says, and out flies a grown-up nightgown. I get frozen. The nightgown smells like the wrong kind of flowers. I don't want to wear it. But Geraldine unbuttons my blouse.

I promise. I promise. I promise. I love you best. Please sober up and come find me.

Geraldine pulls my blouse off. She tugs on my skirt. She scrunches the nightgown right up to the hole in its neck, and the neck slides over my head.

Geraldine thinks I'm a baby. She won't let me do anything for myself. She even takes me in the bathroom and sits me on the toilet. Then she tells me to get in bed.

"Come on," she says. "It's cold." I shake my head. Geraldine must be crazy.

I am not getting in any wall bed.

"Look." She bounces on the bed. She yawns fake. "This is so cozy, and we're so tired. Aren't we tired, little girl?"

I run to the door and listen hard for Old Daddy. I put my hand on the knob. I think I hear his feet.

The knob won't turn.

Geraldine's face gets rocky. "He won't come tonight. Tomorrow, maybe. Now get on back here." She makes more skinny eyes at me. Her voice says loud, "Do you know what I'm going through for you? We ate three of this week's eggs. We drank the last of the milk. And I could get in trouble, too. I could be arrested for kidnapping! So don't you be ungrateful."

I try to turn the knob again, but Geraldine jumps up. I turn it quick and the door goes clack and is stuck against the high chain. I don't see Old Daddy in the hall.

I let go of the knob and Geraldine shuts the door. She carries me back to the bed. "That's a good little girl," she says. "I could use a little girl as good as you."

She makes me lay down. I lay straight, with my stomach squeezed. Any minute the bed will snap shut. Then I'll be like Old Daddy's friend the Angel, all twisted up and buried in concrete.

One-Armed Doll

"My sister tried to steal her. She picked her up and wouldn't let go. She was walking out the door. 'This is the prettiest baby I've ever seen,' she said. 'Just like a baby doll. If I thought I could have me a baby as pretty as this one, I'd go on home and have her.'"

Old Daddy! I open my eyes and there he is, sitting on Geraldine's couch. Jamie stands beside him. The sun is fat in the window. Old Daddy's hat is pushed back on his head and his eyes are crinkled shut. He laughs big when he sees me, and then he pulls his hat back down.

"She's a good little girl," says Geraldine. "An angel." She's sitting on the couch right next to Old Daddy, and she laughs when Old Daddy laughs. Her hand crawls up his arm.

My tongue tastes funny, like sucking on a penny. The grown-up nightgown is tangly when I sit up.

Jamie runs over and hugs me.

"Isn't that the sweetest thing," says Geraldine. "He missed his sister."

Jamie hugs extra tight and won't let go. His heart goes *thump thump thump* with mine. "I didn't want to leave you," he whispers. "Daddy said he would carry me and then come back for you. Only we fell asleep." The way Jamie looks, he wants to cry. "Were you scared?"

I nod my head. I like how he's hugging me.

"Baby Doll," Old Daddy says, "come give your old man one of those."

Jamie tugs my hand until I get out of the wall bed. The tangly nightgown makes me trip. We go over to Old Daddy. He has wide arms like he loves me a lot, but I don't have wide arms back. I stand still until Jamie pushes. Then I hug Old Daddy.

"You scared me to death," Old Daddy says. He looks like Jamie, wanting to cry. "Who's your daddy?"

"You are," I say even before Jamie nudges. Now I like Old Daddy's hug, sort of.

"I didn't mean to put you out." Old Daddy talks to Geraldine, and his chin bumps on my head. His chin digs in, and Geraldine says, "She wasn't any trouble. Like having one of my own."

I push my head up, into Old Daddy's chin. I don't want him talking to Geraldine anymore. I want him to talk to me. But it's too late—Old Daddy is talking and talking to Geraldine. He lets me go. I can't stand the tangly nightgown and have to pull it off.

Jamie helps me find my skirt and blouse. But I won't let him do my zipper; I won't let him do my buttons. Even when I get the buttons wrong I don't want Jamie to help. Then we look at Geraldine's storybook dolls.

"Here," says Geraldine when she sees us looking. She opens a table drawer.

Jamie and I peek in. A doll is lying there, a black-haired doll in a crumpled dress. The dress is colored like lima beans, which I hate. She's not fancy like the dolls on the shelf. Her hair is coming unglued and her arm is gone. Her sleeves have wearing-off glitter and her shoes are only painted on. She looks so sad she makes me sad, too.

"You want to hold her?" says Geraldine. "You can hold her."

Jamie looks at Old Daddy. "Pick her up, Cassie," Jamie says. So I pick her up. I feel the bump of her missing arm and the crumples in her dress. Then I let Jamie feel her.

"Is she glass?" Jamie says.

"Porcelain." Geraldine shuts the table drawer. "Go on and take her. She's got that arm gone. I don't want her anymore."

Swear

When we get back to Diamond Street, Jamie makes me swear on the Holy Bible I won't tell Mama about Geraldine. He says to hide the one-armed doll. I sneak her out of my purse and into the cigar box New Daddy gave me. I put my new Jackson in there too, so it's safe with the old one.

Jamie says never take the doll out. That if Mama finds out I went home with Geraldine, she won't let Old Daddy take us anywhere ever again.

"But what if Mama asks did I stay right with Old Daddy?" I say. "If I say yes, that's a lie."

"It's not a lie," says Jamie, "it's a white lie."

Only I don't know what a white lie is. "A white lie is okay to tell," says Jamie. "Telling a white lie keeps from hurting people's feelings."

But then when Mama asks, "Did you tell me everything you did?" and I say, "Yes, Mama," the white lie hurts inside of me. Like I'm the one-armed doll stuck in a cigar box. Jamie says white is all the colors in the world mixed together, but I don't see other colors in white. When I don't tell Mama and I don't tell Mama about Geraldine, I just see white by itself, like the light on the sidewalk when it burns my eyes.

I still can't tell the truth, though, because of Jamie. When we said goodbye to Old Daddy, Jamie cried and hugged Old Daddy's neck. He told Old Daddy he wants to live with him.

"Aw, what kind of life is this for a kid?" Old Daddy said. He was crying himself. He gave us both wet kisses. I hugged Old Daddy's neck and my stomach felt squished inside, like a big foot was stomping around in there. And I wondered if I have to love my daddy best, like I promised, just because he's my daddy?

I want Jamie to have Old Daddy so he won't be sad, and Old Daddy says we're his children forever and ever. But I don't think I like him very much.

But if Old Daddy knows I don't like him, next time he might just take Jamie away and not me. On Diamond Street I play with Kim Candy from across the street, who is almost my age and wears two pigtails, but Jamie's still my best friend in the world. He knows things nobody else ever knows, and he can do things nobody else can do. Like climb our new fence and hop onto the roof, or run and turn three cartwheels in a row.

Plus he tells me about a French Revolution, where people had to live with the rats crawling over them in a place called a Bastille. He tells me how they cut off a lady's head so it rolled in a basket and her name was Marie Antoinette. Then he puts on his very own tap shoes that Mama bought him for a surprise, and makes the taps sound fast as a rolling tongue. When he taps on the patio, sparks happen under his shoes.

Caught

"Sikes!" Mama is mad at Old Daddy on the phone. "I can't believe this. I can't believe you left her again!" She's strangling my one-armed doll.

I'm crying because Jamie won't listen to me. I try to say I didn't tell on purpose. Mama just opened my door. And then she saw the doll, so I had to tell, because where would I get a porcelain doll? But Jamie's eyes look black, which is no-color, just a big hole you can't see into. He bumps me hard, running into his room, and his door slams shut.

"I'll kill you, Sikes," Mama is yelling. "I'll kill you!" It sounds like she means it. But I know she won't. Now I know that is just something grown-ups say.

Traitor

Jamie stays mad about the one-armed doll. He won't play with me anymore. After school, I watch for him to come home around the corner where Diamond Street flattens out, but he fools me. He comes from uphill, where Diana lives. Uphill the houses shrink and disappear and more people are building fences so you can't see the backyards now. You have to climb up and look over the top, which we aren't supposed to do.

I run to meet Jamie, but he's holding Diana's hand. Diana has green green eyes and chopped yellow hair she's always fluffing.

"Go away," says Jamie. "I don't want you here."

"Me either," Diana says.

Then they play Cleopatra and Mark Antony. Diana gets

to be Cleopatra and Jamie is Mark Antony. Cleopatra wears jewels. Jamie gives Diana a red stone from Mama's jewelry box. He tapes it to her forehead. He wraps her in Mama's old drapes with a cord for a belt, and he wraps himself in old drapes, too. I say I'll tell about him dressing up if they don't let me play, so finally Jamie says I can. But I have to be the slave girl.

I ask for drapes to wear, but Jamie says no. "You're in the dungeon, Cassie. Go stand on the front porch."

"I don't want to be in the dungeon," I say. "I don't want to be the slave girl."

"Too bad," says Jamie and he pushes me. The way he pushes makes everything smudgy, like I'm still tangled up in Geraldine's nightgown and can't get out.

"That's what happens to traitors," Jamie says.

Toy Soldier

Jamie dances the Little Toy Soldier again, for a talent show at school. On the day he dances, he gets to go late so Mama can drive him all dressed up. There's a stage set up in a big room where you eat. Jamie says he doesn't want me to watch, but Mama says I can.

She puts me in the front row with the kindergartners, which I will be pretty soon. She gives me a green paper with the names of all the talent-show kids written down, and she draws a star by Jamie's name so I can find him.

First there are girls throwing batons and doing the Hula-Hoop, then a boy who plays flute. None of them are half as good as Jamie.

When Jamie comes out he stands high on the stage, special in his soldier suit and hat. His cheeks are red with Mama's makeup and his eyes are outlined black. He looks all around except at me. Then he hears the music how he does, even before it starts, and I can feel him listening. When the real music comes on, his feet make a happy tapping noise all around the room.

"That's Jamie. That's my brother!" I tell the girl right next to me.

Jamie's so good, he wins the talent-show prize, which is a ticket for an ice cream sundae. He comes back on stage to collect, but it's funny, because hardly any of the children clap. You can hear them not clapping across the room, a sound like an engine that has gotten stuck.

Mama says I should walk home from school with Jamie to learn the way. Jamie is so happy he won the prize, he forgets I'm a traitor and says okay. He's so happy I don't tell him nobody clapped. I don't say anything until I see the boys. Big boys with smirky faces, walking up fast behind us.

"I'm going to be famous!" goes Jamie. "I'll be on TV." He isn't wearing his Toy Soldier suit now, but there's still black stuff on his eyes.

"Jamie," I say.

"Just like Reece," says Jamie.

"Jamie!"

"What?"

It's too late. Now I can hear the boy's panting noises. "Hey, sissy. Hey, fag," they say, their lips going *kiss kiss kiss*.

I don't know what a fag is, but I know they're being mean.

Jamie isn't smiling now. He grabs my hand like I'm not a traitor after all and we walk faster together. But the boys walk faster, too. They get so close they run ahead and make a circle walking around us. I see Winston and Matt from next door, and right away I don't like them anymore.

A snarly-faced boy gurgles, and out sails a spit glob. Winston walks behind us and steps on Jamie's heels. Jamie's shoe comes off and his sock falls down. There's a red mark on his skin.

I feel wrinkled inside. I look for Diamond Street and our house, but I don't see it. I don't know where we are. The boys won't stop following. They scrunch in close and Jamie jerks my hand. Matt runs in front of us and tries to pretend he's tap-dancing. His feet clunk the road.

"You don't know anything!" Jamie says. And I think Jamie's right.

"I know what a fag is," says the spit-glob boy. He points at Jamie, and his point is like a stick in me, jabbing. "Hey," he says, "look what I found." He steals Jamie's bubble gum out of his pocket, the good kind wrapped in tiny comics. I hear a screaming sound from my head.

"Give that back," Jamie shouts. But the spit-glob boy just laughs. He throws the tiny comics on the lawn. He sticks the gum in his spitty mouth and chews.

"Let's fight," he says.

"I don't want to."

"Chicken!" The boy makes chicken noises. *Bawk. Bawk. Bawk.* His elbows flap up and down.

"You're just stupid," Jamie says.

Spit Glob gets a pumpkin grin and pokes Jamie some more. Jamie slaps his hand, but he pokes and pokes to make us go

70

up on somebody's lawn, even though we don't want to go. "Where's your little toy gun, soldier? Aren't you scared without it?" he says.

Jamie looks worried at me. He can't keep hold of my hand. Even Matt looks worried now, and the screaming sound in my head won't stop.

"Come on, chicken," says Spit Glob. He punches Jamie's face. *Smack*. Jamie's cheek goes white and then red and the screaming sound in my head comes out.

"No, no, no!" I shout and kick the spit-glob boy. His face snaps and he pushes me backwards until I'm flying over the lawn.

"Leave her alone!" says Jamie, and he tries to punch Spit Glob. But he can't punch him very hard.

"Got your little sister to protect you, faggot?" Spit Glob says, and then he pushes Jamie down, too.

"Run, Cassie!" Jamie cries. I jump up from the lawn, but I don't know where to run. The green paper is in the gutter, wet. I see the star by Jamie's name. One of the boys is stepping on it, but they're not paying any attention to me.

I run and run and run until I find Diamond Street. Then I run to our house. When I tell her, Mama says, "Get in the car," and drives so fast I bump my shoulder. "Where?" she shouts. "Where are they?"

We turn the corner and then I see the boys. I see Spit Glob with his knee on Jamie's back. He's rubbing Jamie's face in the grass.

Mama honks the horn and hollers. "Get away! Get away from him!" The car jumps right up on the lawn and Mama hops out and keeps on hollering. She goes for Spit Glob, but she misses him because he's already running away.

Jamie sits up. His face is hurt and grassy.

"Got your mama now?" Spit Glob says, skipping backwards up the street.

"Your mother's going to hear about this!" Mama calls. "Yours, too." She points at Winston and Matt.

"Jamie?" she says. "What did they do? Did they hurt you?"

Jamie stands up and Mama puts her arms around him. But Jamie claws away. "Don't!" he says, looking for the boys. "Leave me alone." He wipes his eyes. He goes over to the car and climbs in.

Baseball

New Daddy teaches Jamie baseball. I want to learn, but Mama says just watch them from the lawn, baseball is a boy thing. So I pretend I'm playing while I watch.

Jamie wears New Daddy's old mitt, and the mitt is big on his hand. He fiddles and fiddles with it and he isn't ready when New Daddy tosses him the ball.

"Watch out!" I say, and "Again," New Daddy calls. The next time Jamie catches it. Then New Daddy shows him how to step and throw—from his shoulder, not his elbow. And I step and throw my pretend ball, too, but it's not the same as being Jamie and playing with New Daddy.

New Daddy is rolling the push mower across the lawn. The grass jumps up behind him and sticks to his ankles and shoes. Winston and Matt from next door run out. "Don't slam the door!" their crazy mother shouts, when it's too late. They slam the door.

New Daddy stops the push mower. "They're waiting for you to play ball," he tells Jamie.

"But I hate them," Jamie says. "They're only doing it because they got in trouble."

"You might make some friends." New Daddy says boys make friends playing ball.

I ask to push the mower, so he lets me, but only until Mama comes out. "Be careful!" Mama says. "If you got your feet under the blades they could slice your toes off." I'm not that dumb, but she won't believe me. Then I don't have anything to do, so I sit by the gutter waiting for the baseball game to start.

"They're never going to like me," Jamie says when he comes over. He splats his shoes in the gutter water.

When I say, "Daddy says they will," Jamie looks mad at me.

"*Ellis* thinks I'm a sissy, too," he says.

"No, he doesn't."

"What do you know? You like him better than you like your real daddy."

"No, I don't."

"Yes, you do. That's why you told about Geraldine. That's why I'm stuck here on Diamond Street. Because of you!"

"He'll come back," I say. "I bet he does."

"If he does, then I'm leaving forever. And this time you can't come." Jamie splats the water hard. His mad look goes over to New Daddy and Mama, watching.

"Maybe I don't want to!" I say.

"Fine," says Jamie, and he scrapes his shoes walking slow to the street.

All the boys from Diamond Street are playing. Winston and Matt and Sam Candy and Louis from three doors down.

They play in the street. Home base is a chalk square, and so is second. Our little tree is first, and Janet Candy's parked car makes third.

Matt is catcher and Winston pitches. He throws to Jamie and Jamie swings. He misses. Winston pitches again. Jamie nicks the ball and it goes flying and lands smack inside Matt's mitt.

Then Jamie tries again. This time he hits the ball and throws the bat and runs. The bat bounces and rolls. Winston scoops up the ball and chases him. But Jamie gets to base first.

"You're out!" yells Winston.

"I'm not!" says Jamie. "I'm safe!"

Winston looks at Matt and Matt says, "Out."

"Out. Out," says Louis from three doors down. Sam Candy shrugs, and Jamie's face gets red. He pushes Winston.

"Oh, yeah?" says Winston and pushes back. A car comes by and nobody moves. The car honks, and all the boys rush to the grass and watch it. Jamie walks away, and Winston tosses the ball to Matt right over the moving car.

I run up to our house, where Mama is saying to New Daddy, "I want to fix the front of the house. We'll put a rock garden here, and a palm tree. We'll set gardenias under the window." And I tug on her blouse and point out Jamie, who's down at the corner, sitting on the grass with his head on his knees. Anybody can see he's crying.

Baby Boys

"No more dress-up," New Daddy tells Jamie. "No more dolls. You can come in the garage and help me work."

Jamie doesn't want to. He runs and hides around the side of the house and New Daddy has to find him.

"I do it, too," I tell Mama. "I dress up. I get in your things. I want to help in the garage."

"I've told you Ellis wants a boy to help," Mama says. "You can help me here." She's folding clothes from the basket. I pick up a shirt and look at her stomach again. Mama says, "Not yet." And when I hope for a girl she says, "No, you don't want a sister. Believe me—I had eight of them. Besides, a boy would make Ellis so happy."

Jamie says the baby won't be our real brother or sister anyway, just half. But Mama says that's nonsense, that we're a family now.

Summer Christmas

Everything is upside down. The witch won't let New Daddy have his children for Christmas, so we are going to make Christmas come in summer, when Jamie is out of school. And I thought New Daddy only had two children, but now he has three. Sarah, Davey, and a bigger girl called April.

I don't know what to say to them. We all go into the front yard listening for the ice cream man to come. I like Sarah best. She's littler than me and has soft yellow hair. When she sits on New Daddy's lap her curls fit around his big fingers. She wears suits without legs that have skinny strings to tie at the shoulders. I wish Mama would buy me a suit like that, and I'm going to ask her to curl my hair.

Davey is older than me but not as old as Jamie. When he

sees no one is looking, he hits Jamie's arm. April, who is way older than Davey, tells him not to hit, but she isn't watching when she says it. She's making dreamy eyes at Diamond Street, holding the ice cream money in her hand. She wears pants that don't come all the way to her ankles and a top that doesn't come all the way to her belly. There's a ruffle along the neck of her top. She twists a tube of pink lipstick and pulls color around her mouth, smushes her lips together, and asks Jamie about Winston, from next door.

I hear the ice cream man coming. The music sounds like bells, and you can tell when he stops from the way the sound goes round and round but not forward. I want a Drumstick but they cost more than Missiles, so Mama says we have to get Missiles when New Daddy's children are here.

Jamie still won't play with me. He goes in the backyard with April and says I'm too little to come. He and April climb the fence and peek into Winston's yard. Mama says, "What can you do? All the girls like Jamie." She says, "Davey is going to help Daddy in the garage, and you can play with Sarah."

I play with Sarah all day, and then I have to share the company room with her at night, because April sleeps in my bed. Sarah wiggles in the big bed, not going to sleep. She calls and calls until New Daddy comes in and turns on the light. But Sarah isn't scared he'll be mad. She grabs his neck and holds him extra tight. She looks at him and her eyes are round and perfectly brown, and her cheeks have dents like New Daddy's cheeks when he smiles. New Daddy makes his nose kiss her nose in a game they play.

I get up and go in the bathroom. I look in the mirror at my cheeks, but there are no dents in them. And my eyes are not round and perfectly brown. They have lots of other colors. I think about the white lie I didn't tell Mama, burning in my eyes until she found it. I think how I got Jamie stuck on Diamond Street. I think how I have two daddies, and I don't know which one is really mine.

The shower door is two pieces of glass with tiny wires in wavy squares. I scrunch on the floor and watch the wires the way they worm in the milky glass until I'm sure that Sarah is asleep.

The Train

On summer Christmas morning the train is big across the living room floor. There's an engine and a caboose and three cars in between to be the boxcars, and all of them are big enough to sit in. They hook together and they each have wheels. The engine has a little hood and smokestack just like a real engine. It's got a bell to ring and a pretend light on front above its engine teeth. The caboose has another roof with a smokestack, and both rooftops are painted red, like the wheels.

Me and Jamie and April and Sarah and Davey all stand staring. Then Davey runs over to the engine and jumps in. Jamie runs over too, and stands beside him, watching him ring the bell.

"Everybody in for the movie," New Daddy says. He tells us to go in order of our ages, which means April will be in the engine, because she's oldest.

"I don't want to change places!" Davey whines.

"Come on, son." New Daddy waves his movie camera. He's already turned on the row of big lights that make your eyes squinch.

"Okay, but only if I can get right back in." Davey climbs out with his eyes stuck on the engine. New Daddy tells Mama to hold the camera while he pulls us around the room, April in front, with Jamie next, then Davey, then me, and then Sarah, who gets the caboose.

"I hope I'm getting it right. I hope I'm getting it," Mama keeps saying. She says the train is the cutest thing in the whole wide world. After a while New Daddy takes the camera back and tries to get her picture.

"Ellis!" Mama screams. "I haven't fixed my face yet." Everybody laughs about Mama fixing her face because it sounds like something else, but it means putting her makeup on. And when we laugh it feels so happy together.

Davey wants to ride in the engine again. He wants to ride in it all the time, and won't let anybody else. Jamie stands with his arms crossed until New Daddy makes Davey give him a turn. Then Davey takes the caboose so I have to stay in one of the plain cars. I don't ever get the engine.

"I'm going to take this train home, can I, Daddy?" Davey asks.

I stop my breath. New Daddy rubs his slicked-back hair down to the back of his neck. "I made it for all of you. You can play with it when you come over."

"That's not the same!" says Davey.

"What if you take some of the cars, then, and we'll keep the rest?"

"All right," Davey says, "but I get the engine."

New Daddy rubs the back of his neck again.

"I helped make the engine," Jamie says. "Once."

"So, he's my dad," says Davey. "And I helped, too."

"It's Christmas," Mama says. "Let's share."

"I know," says April in her I'm-the-oldest voice. "We should each keep the car we rode in first, when Daddy took the movie."

I don't feel like laughing now. I cross my arms like Jamie and stare at her. My heart goes fast. If we do that, Jamie and me won't get anything but the plain cars, since Sarah was in the caboose.

"That's not fair, is it?" Jamie cries. He runs over to Mama. I run over to Mama, too.

"Well, no, not exactly," Mama says. She looks at New Daddy. "Let's open our other presents now. We can worry about this later."

I get an ironing board and a tea set and a new doll, but I wish I could have that train engine instead, even though I know by now that Davey will be the one to get it.

Mama won't let me go with Sarah when her mother the witch comes to take them home. She won't let me spend the night at Sarah's house, even though Sarah spent all those nights with us.

"That's different," Mama says.

Sarah doesn't want to get in the car. She cries and cries like Jamie cries saying goodbye to Old Daddy, and she hugs New Daddy's neck. That makes April cry, and Davey.

New Daddy sits out on the front porch a long time after they drive away. "Leave him alone," says Mama. "He misses his kids." Then I wish I could really be New Daddy's kid, so he could miss me, too.

Mama curls my hair with a brush and water the first day of kindergarten. She twirls me to the mirror. "You look like an angel," she says. "I love that pink dress. The lace is so pretty on the collar."

But I don't want to be an angel. I run to the window so I can watch Jenny Field, who lives on the corner and is a year older than me, come out in her black-and-red-checked skirt. She's got on knee socks, which Mama won't let me wear. Her sweater is dark blue. Her hair is braided, but Mama won't let me have braids, either.

"Can I have a skirt like that?" I ask.

"That old thing? That's a uniform, honey, for the Catholic school. Who'd wear an old drab uniform if they didn't have to? Now stay clean. I'll be getting ready."

Mama leaves the room. I take my pink dress off and put on my orange one instead. The orange is plain with a black ribbon in front. I come out and Mama's dressing our new baby, Nick. "You don't have to come," I say.

"What are you talking about? We're taking you to school." She looks funny at me in the orange dress.

"But I want to walk with Jamie."

"Where's your pink dress?"

"Only babies have their mama take them to school."

Mama slips a little white bootie on Baby Nick and kisses his fat knee. "But I've always wanted to take my little girl to kindergarten. I'm your mother, remember?" Baby Nick spits up goo and she wipes his chin.

"I don't want you to."

"Where'd my little girl go?" says Mama like she's lost me.

Then she lifts Baby Nick and lays him on his blanket in his playpen. Her hair falls across her eyes. "Did you see my bobby pin?" she says. "It's not in the playpen, is it?" She shakes and shakes the blankets. She pokes around in his toys. "I've got to find it, Cassie; he could choke on something like that." I help her find the bobby pin, which is lying on the floor. "Thank God," says Mama. She jiggles Baby Nick.

"Mama?"

"Oh, all right, if that's the way you're going to be. But you have to stay right with Jamie. You have to hold his hand."

"I will." I run outside and Mama makes us be in a picture in front of the house, me and Jamie pretending to step out the door, our hands on the knob. She takes us by the little tree, squinting into the sun. I run back in and talk to Baby Nick.

"I'll only be gone for a little while," I tell him. "I'll be back pretty soon. Watch out for bobby pins." I don't really mind that he's a boy. He has serious eyes and smiles around his bottle, which Mama has got stuck on his chest with a little turtle pillow. Elastic comes out of the turtle to hold the bottle for him. Usually I hold it, but I won't be here today.

Mama cries when she waves goodbye. "Don't talk to strangers," she says. "Stay right with Jamie. Don't get in anybody's car!" I can hear her voice almost to the end of Diamond Street.

Walking to school we cross four streets and turn a corner, and end where the gates meet on each side of the path. The path goes long between two playing fields. After the fields comes blacktop, and then some low buildings start.

"The principal has no arm," says Jamie. "Just like that old doll. He spanks you with a board."

I stare down the path. It's hard and brown with tiny white rocks in the dirt, so that if you fall in a dress you'll scrape your knees and have to pick the rocks out. There's a fence all around the school, but it doesn't make me feel safe. I bet I could climb it if I had to.

"Come on." Jamie runs down the path. When we get to the buildings he takes me to the kindergarten. There's no garden like I thought and it's caged off from the other rooms, with a sandbox and swings in the cage. I follow Jamie back out into the regular hall.

"What are you doing?" Jamie looks around but not at me.

"I want to stay with you until the bell rings." I know all about the bells from Jamie.

"You can't."

Some boys are coming down the hall. They bump into Jamie but they don't say *Hello* or *Excuse me*. Then they laugh and walk away.

"I don't want you following me," Jamie says.

"Why not?"

"You know why. Go back to kindergarten, Cassie. I mean it."

Jamie is still watching those boys. When they aren't looking, he runs off and turns a corner fast. I have to run to catch him. I grab his arm but Jamie jerks away. He pushes me and I land on the lawn between two classrooms. "I said get out of here!" he yells.

I don't want to cry on the first day of school. I go back to the kindergarten without Jamie.

My teacher has a flowy dress. She smiles at me and opens the door. "Where's your mother?" she says, but I don't tell her. "Scared?" she says, but I'm not scared. The other children have all brought their mothers and some of them cry and grab their mothers' legs.

Jamie is right about the principal. He only has one arm. Where his other arm should be is just a sleeve folded over. We listen to him say some words out by the flagpole. The teacher lines us up and tells us to salute, which is putting a hand over your heart while the principal talks.

We have two flags, a red, white, and blue one with stars and a white one with a bear. When Jamie has nightmares he sees a big black bear out the window, but this bear looks friendly, bending in the sky. The cord clacks the flagpole.

I'm afraid to look at the principal's missing arm. I wonder if it hurts and where they put it when it came off. I can't see how he can spank anyone with only one arm. How would he keep you from running away?

I want to tell Jamie this, in case he gets sent to the principal. I look for him with the other second graders. He's standing at the end of a row in back. His hand is over his heart. A boy pulls on his ear and Jamie shoves his hand away. He's not looking for me at all.

Another One

All day Mama makes the house look pretty. When New Daddy comes home from work, Mama comes out of the kitchen and they kiss big in the hall. Then Mama's face gets red. "Cassie's watching," she says, even though I always shut my eyes. When I open my eyes he kisses her again. He lifts me up until my shoes are on top of his boots, where I feel big even if my arms can hardly reach. "Hold on," he says, and flies me backwards around the room. He whistles and sings, *"When the red-red robin comes bob-bob-bobbin along!"*

Jamie comes inside and New Daddy turns him sideways. He holds Jamie's hand and leg and Jamie is an airplane, flying. Then Jamie gets dizzy and New Daddy sets him down and does gorilla arms and teeth. Jamie and I scream and run, and the gorilla chases us until we jump over the couch to hide. New Daddy roars, and in the playpen Baby Nick kicks and smiles.

"That's not your real daddy," Kim Candy says to me. "Your brother said so." She stomps in the gutter water with her bare feet, which Mama says never to do but I don't see why.

I take my sandals off and put my feet in next to hers. "Jamie's a liar. That is too my daddy."

"That's not what he told my mama. He said you have another daddy and Ellis is a step."

"He's not a step. Jamie's lying!"

"Is he mean?"

"No."

"My daddy is mean. He hits us with a big wood spoon," says Kim Candy. "Do you want to come over and play?"

All the number-three houses on Diamond Street look alike, but different things happen in them. In Kim Candy's house, the shades are pulled down tight. The air is gray. Janet Candy sits on a stool and smokes right into the telephone.

She doesn't worry about making her house pretty. She has spills on the rug and dirty dishes in the sink. The table has something sticky on it when I put my elbow there. There are magazines slidey under my feet, and nobody makes their bed.

Sam Candy runs by and pinches me. "Sam! Knock it off or else!" yells Janet Candy, but she doesn't move.

Kim pulls me into her room. There are toys everywhere, heaps of toys between papers and shirts and jackets and shoes. I don't see how she can find anything, and how they keep from getting broken.

"I know a secret," she says. "You won't tell?"

"I won't tell. I know lots of secrets," I say.

"Promise on the holy Bible?"

"On the holy Bible." Jamie must have taught her that.

Kim yanks her shirt up and one side of her chest is funny. The skin is purple and splotchy, with dents in it. "I got burnt," she says, "so I can't grow a titty."

Just like the man who was burnt in the alley behind our brown-grass house. The man with staring eyes and no hair and blotchy skin. "Did it hurt?"

"Mama says it was hot soup." She touches her blotchy skin. Then she yanks her shirt back down. "My mama's got titties," she says, "big ones."

"That's a bad word," I say, even though Old Daddy says it all the time.

That makes Kim giggle and I do too. "Titties! Titties!" she says. I stick my hand over her mouth and she screams behind it, "Titties! Titties!" until her door flies open.

Mama and Janet Candy are standing there. "Cassie!" Mama says. "What are you doing over here? Don't ever go somewhere without telling me."

I jump up. "I'm sorry, Mama."

"I was worried to death!"

"Good grief, Belle," says Janet Candy. "We're just across the street."

Mama doesn't answer. Her face gets bunchy and she runs into the bathroom and throws up. Kim and I run after her, but Janet Candy tells us to stay back. She wets a towel for Mama's head and wrings it in the sink.

"Queasy," Mama says. Her hands are shaking.

Janet Candy pats her stomach. "You too?" she says.

"Oh, God," says Mama. She sits on the toilet and bends over her knees. "The kids don't know it yet."

"Know what?" I say.

"Oh, honey." Mama's voice is hard to hear, bent over like that. "I'm going to have another baby. Isn't that wonderful?"

"Then why are you sick?"

Mama's head comes up. "It might be a girl. Girls can make you sick at first."

"Did I make you sick at first?"

"Of course not," Mama says, but I don't believe her.

"Come sit on the couch," says Janet Candy.

Mama gets off the toilet and we all follow. "Jesus," she says, "I didn't know it would be like this."

"Here, try this." Janet Candy gives Mama a beer. "Is it planned?"

"Of course." Mama rolls the beer bottle across her forehead. "At least—we want it."

"Diapers and late nights? Swollen tits? I wish I didn't have to go through it again." Janet Candy drinks her own beer, and Kim and I giggle because she said tits, too.

Mama pulls my hand until I'm standing close. "Cassie will help, won't you, baby?" she says. And I say yes because I feel happy when Mama counts on me.

Ship in a Bottle

In the garage New Daddy's storage boxes are full of dusty stuff. He cleans them out on Saturday, and this time I get to help because I have my play clothes on. He opens a metal box and inside are the tiniest seashells in the world, all polished and perfect. In a bigger box is a rubber suit to go under water, a rifle, and a tin of bullets and a fishing pole. More hammers and saws and nails. Then we find the strangest thing. A ship that sailed right into a bottle.

"I made it," New Daddy says when I say how did it get in there. "Someday I'll make a real one, too. Just like that." New Daddy's eyes look somewhere else; then his eyes come back and he starts to whistle. "Your mama and I will sail away," he says.

"Can I come too?" I don't want New Daddy and Mama to sail away without me. "And Nick and Jamie and the new baby?"

New Daddy stops his whistle. He pulls my nose off and shows me it's between his fingers again. "I'd never leave you kids behind," he says.

Egg Plate

On the phone Old Daddy's voice sounds far away. "Baby Doll," he shouts, "how are you?" so I know he's walking haywire. I try to tell him how I am, but my heart goes like it's been running too fast.

"Tell him you're in kindergarten now. Ask him when he's coming to see you," Mama whispers in my ear.

"Are you going to take Jamie away?" I ask.

"What?" Old Daddy says. "I can't come now. I've got a lot of work. A new territory to cover. Your old man's selling garbage disposals. You put in your carrots and potato peels, right down this hole in the sink. Then you turn it on, and *presto*, they disappear! I sold so many I'm top man this month. Boss gave me a present I'm saving for you."

Over my shoulder Mama tries to listen. She puts her ear next to my ear. "He's got a present," I say. I can't remember Old Daddy giving me a present before. I wonder what it will be.

"Tell him he can visit you here," says Mama. "No more outings."

"A disposal is a powerful machine," Old Daddy says. "It could take your fingers off if you stuck them inside."

"Say Jamie misses him," goes Mama. "A lot."

"So sad, too bad, your dad," Old Daddy says for goodbye. "Send me your school papers now." He kisses the air for me and it's like I can feel his pokey cheek.

I have a bad dream. *I'm on the storybook-doll shelf at Geraldine's, but Old Daddy won't take me down. He's mad because I didn't give him his Jackson back.*

In school the teacher says write your name across the top of the paper, and when I write Cassie she says, "No, I mean your daddy's name." But I don't know which daddy she means. Then she looks in a book and tells me my last name is Worth, for Ellis Worth. W-O-R-T-H, spelled out.

On the way home from school I ask Jamie what his last name is, and he says Mama wants it to be Worth for now. "But it's not really Worth," he says. "We aren't adopted."

"What do you mean?"

"We belong to our real daddy, dimwit. Now run ahead so no one sees us together."

I run home and play with Baby Nick. His eyes have gone from blue to brown, which is something funny like the black worm that came out of his stomach when he was new. Then the black worm fell off.

I think how I'm not adopted. How Baby Nick belongs to Mama and New Daddy the way I used to belong to her and Old Daddy. But I don't really belong to Old Daddy anymore. I'm going to teach Baby Nick right away that his name is W-O-R-T-H, spelled out.

In the morning Mama says Old Daddy was here. There is a blue plate on the table. The plate is funny-shaped, like a flower with cups where the petals should be, and gold paint around the cups. Mama says the plate is the present Old Daddy got me.

"An egg plate," she says. "And we bought one of his garbage disposals, too. But you kids will have to be careful; you can't stick your hands down there."

I already know this, but Mama isn't listening. She's pulling bacon from the pan and lining it up on the towel. The towel looks wet and "Hungry?" she says.

Jamie says no. He tries not to cry because he missed Old Daddy. He wipes his eyes. He doesn't care about the plate. New Daddy comes in the kitchen and I show my plate to him.

"I saw it, Cass." New Daddy looks sad at me.

"Is it real gold?" I ask about the edges.

New Daddy says over my head to Mama, "What kind of a present is that?"

"Ellis—" says Mama.

"I mean it. What kind of a present is that for a kid?"

"Give it here." Mama takes my plate away. "I'll put it up and save it for you."

"Dammit," New Daddy says. "That man should straighten up!"

New Daddy sounds mad, which he doesn't usually, so it makes me scared. He's wearing his long green pants and white shirt for work, and his name is fancy on the pocket. I can read it now.

Mama is holding the bacon fork. "How do you want your eggs?" she asks.

"Why do you defend him?" New Daddy says. "He drank before you left him. He drank for years. Stop feeling guilty."

"I don't."

"Yes, you do."

Mama sets the fork down slow. She looks at me and Jamie. She looks like she wants things the way they used to be, when everything was on the Q.T.

"Sweetheart," New Daddy says and hugs her. "That man should remember that he's their father." And even though he doesn't kiss her, I have to shut my eyes.

A Thought

Here's what I think. I think having two daddies is like riding the elephant. You don't know until you get up there what an elephant smells like, or how high you will be on the elephant's back. But then you realize. And the basket tips one way and then the other, like you might fall, every time the elephant steps.

90

"Don't sign your papers with his last name," Old Daddy whispers over the phone. "You're my Baby Doll! Do you want to hurt your daddy?" He calls us when we're already asleep and I have to hold the phone tight to my ear to keep awake. I think he's haywire again, but I'm not sure. His voice sounds far away. Maybe his new territory is in another country.

I don't know what to do because I already signed my papers.

I hear a lady yelling. Hollering like somebody tied her up and she's trying to wrestle free. Like Jamie when he's trapped and melting in hot lava. "Hang up!" she screams. "Hang up!"

"Who's that?" I say.

"That's my crazy gypsy lady," Old Daddy says. "She lives with me now." My heart snaps. Old Daddy lives with a gypsy lady? "You don't want to meet her," he says. "She's mean as all get-out." But I haven't asked.

I look at Jamie, waiting.

"Traitor," Jamie mouths. And when he's a gypsy stuck in hot lava he says gypsies have special powers and evil ways. They can put a curse on you.

Old Daddy's crazy gypsy lady is putting a curse on me. "Devil in the grass! Devil in the grass!" she yells. "You gonna be sorry now, little girl!"

"Baby Doll!" Old Daddy is yelling, too. "Tough titty said the kitty when the milk ran dry!"

"You gonna be sorry! You gonna be!" the gypsy shouts. "You don't want your daddy's name I put a curse on you!"

"What'd I tell you?" Old Daddy says. "Mean as a snake!" Then the phone goes dead.

Part 2

"Keep your chin up."
—*Ellis*

Little Devils

"Baby Neal," Daddy says behind the clicking of the movie on Saturday night. We're eating popcorn and sitting on the rug. The lights are out. In the movie Mama's hand shows first. On her wrist is the charm bracelet Daddy bought her with a charm for each of us kids—a dancer, a girl's silhouette, a fish, and a lamb. The lamb is for our new baby, Neal, nicknamed Boomer. The charms have our names engraved on them, and they dangle when Mama points. Then comes Boomer's face, pinched and ugly, even though Mama says all her babies come out perfect. Mama tickles him and he smiles. He spits up goo. Mama has dressed him in a white knit suit and matching booties, and his tiny arms go jumpy trying to reach her.

"Little Devils," Daddy says, and now in the movies Nick is two and Boomer's already one. Nick runs all over the house pulling his string toy behind him. He stacks plastic blocks and bangs them over. He calls on his plastic telephone. "Hello! Hello!" Nick shouts silently, and looks into space with his serious eyes. He doesn't want to be held when I come in the picture, but Boomer crawls in my lap and my mouth moves, singing him songs. I remember I sang "Little Red Wagon" and "How Much Is That Doggie in the Window?"

Suddenly Nick wants to be in my lap too, and that makes Boomer mad. He pushes Nick but can't knock him over. Then Nick hits him on the head with one of the plastic blocks and Boomer cries. I watch myself hug Boomer and remember how soft he was and how his tears against my lips tasted like salt. In the movie his chest goes up up up and then down. The plastic pants over his diaper sag. I check to see if he's wet by laying him on his back. I play the game about the big old buzzard so he'll quit fussing. His eyes watch my hand, swooping the air, his eyes are so surprised, and he squeals his happy squeal when the buzzard dives down at the end.

"Small Sailors," Daddy says, and Nick and Boomer are both running now. Nick looks thin and anxious, and Boomer is chubby with dimples and a curl in the middle of his forehead that no amount of water will straighten. They're both dressed in the two little suits Mama made, exactly alike, with long blue sailor pants and sailor shirts with white-edged collars. They even have white sailor hats and little polished Oxfords to wear. They look so funny running around and around the lawn, like short men in baggy pants, heading for important places. Nick rushes ahead and Boomer kicks up his toes stumbling after. For a minute we can see, across the street, Janet Candy's little girl, Carmen, who's the same age as Boomer. "Run it backwards," Jamie begs, because that always makes everyone laugh.

Daddy's newest movies are in color. "Jamie Dancing," he says, and out leaps Jamie, twirling so fast it takes my breath away. But I hate "Cassie at the Piano." I'm not good at the piano, an antique player Mama bought, so I'm glad the movies have no sound. I have to play in one of the look-alike dresses Mama made us. After I play we go outside in our dresses. Mama wants to show them off. Her red hair catches the sun. The dress is white with aqua stripes, and she's draped a white sweater over her shoulders. She's lost all the weight from having babies, and the dress fits tight at the waist and full in the skirt. It bounces at her knee when she walks across the grass, and her sweater slopes just right and doesn't fall.

Mama turns to Daddy, holding the camera, and she looks so happy, blowing him a kiss.

Electric Current

One day Daddy calls everybody into the garage, even Mama and Jamie. He's fixing an old lamp and he sets it on the floor.

"Make a circle," Daddy says, "and hold hands."

"What for?" says Jamie.

"You'll see," Daddy says. Wires leak from the lamp bottom. He plugs in the cord and touches the wires together.

"That will shock you!" Jamie says. But Daddy shakes his head.

He takes my hand and I take Boomer's. Mama holds Nick and finally Jamie grabs on, too.

"Are you going to shock us?" Nick says.

Daddy grins. He hits the wires together again, in his hand holding mine. His other hand catches Jamie's and then we're all holding hands.

"We're a human electric current machine!" Daddy laughs. "Feel it?"

"I feel it!" I say. The tingle zings through his hand into mine and shoots out of me into Boomer. I look at Mama and Nick and Jamie, and I know they can feel it, zinging through them, too. Mama was right. We're a family now.

Sometimes I still fly in my dreams. I fall asleep and the bed starts to spin. *It spins and spins like a top driving right up through the ceiling, until the bed melts away and I'm in the night sky, going fast. I whiz past the Sears store where the white horse used to run; I whiz past the river that River City is named for. The wind lifts my hair and rushes into my ears like music.*

But sometimes I have the bad dream, and I sleepwalk. Sometimes I get stomachaches. Mama says I dream so much because my tonsils are as big as golf balls and I need to have them out. She says growing pains cause the stomachaches. But inside my bad dream it's always the same. *I'm the doll on Geraldine's shelf. I'm tangled in her nightgown so I can't get down.* Her *voice is everywhere, Old Daddy's crazy gypsy lady. The loud, sharp way she sounds on the phone, only worse, telling me she knows. She knows that we're a family. That I love my new daddy better. I broke my promise, and someday I'll have to pay.*

The End of the World

The River City newspaper said Psychic Predicts Friday Will Be End of the World. I look down the school path, but I don't step through the gates. It's going to rain. The sky is fat close clouds. It's windy. The path looks like forever until the asphalt starts. I'm almost late for third grade; only one or two kids are still on the playground, chasing balls. If I hurry I can make it before I get a red mark. But I don't move. If it's really the end of the world I want to go home.

The newspaper says it will happen with floods and earthquakes, but I think the end of the world will start with the atom bomb. I know all about the A-bomb from watching Japanese movies on TV. The Japanese remember what it's like because a real A-bomb dropped on them. In the end of the world soldiers run around the dark streets with blaring microphones on top of vans. They warn people away from the monsters created by radiation.

Radiation made the giant bird Rodan and the man who wouldn't stop growing and the man who wouldn't stop shrinking. It made the killer crabs and ruined the mushroom people's skin, and it left the dead quiet streets full of awful sun where only trash moves in the wind.

I wish we had a bomb shelter. Mama never reads the papers, and she laughs when I tell her about the end of the world. "Of all the things to worry about," she says. "There's worse things, I'll clue you." But she won't tell me what the worse things are.

In school we practice filing into the cafeteria when the alarm sounds. The principal explains that we might have to stay here together in an emergency, and he tells us how to behave. He says we won't be allowed to go home if this happens, and that we must act like a family together. "You just come on home anyway," Mama says.

Karen Sly says she'll run home, too. She lives next door to the school and her father buried a shelter for them. When they tore down the fence to get the machines through, I watched them scoop out the earth and set the long metal room down. Then they covered it over. The door to the metal room comes up out of the grass now. Inside is filled with canned food and water to keep it safe from fallout. But Karen's mother says she wishes they could have gotten a swimming pool instead.

I picture Karen Sly and her mother and father and sister safe under the earth in their bomb shelter. If they heard us moaning and crying, would they open their door and make room? They'd run out of food, trying to share it with everyone. They'd run out of space. We'll never get a bomb shelter of our own. Mama wants a swimming pool, too, and she says she'd take that over a tin can in the ground any day.

My skin feels crawly, and I jump when the final bell rings. Rain shoots tiny sideways pricks across the path. There aren't any more kids left on the playground. Now I'll get a red mark for sure, and look dumb going in late. I step out on the path. There's a gush of wind like someone following me. I walk a little way and look again. No one. But it could be the principal. He paddles anyone he catches skipping school. And it doesn't matter if he doesn't have his second arm to hold you, he holds you with his eyes. And nobody but Jamie was ever brave enough to try and run away from him.

Now the sound is closer, like a tiger growling. It's not someone following me on the path, but in the sky. A plane! I've never seen one like it before. It's got funny wings and no windows, and it moves faster than a shadow. Whoever is in there can see me perfectly.

My heart feels shoved into my temples. My eyes are stuck to the plane. It flies over the school like a giant bullet. At the last minute it rockets straight up and roars louder than any noise I've heard before. Louder than thunder. And a terrible boom and everything shakes.

I turn and run for home as fast as I can.

I run down Berryfield to Fallen Leaf and have to stop at the corner of Diamond Street because the pain is too sharp in my side. I can't get my breath and it hurts to suck in air. I can't help it; I start to cry. And Old Daddy's crazy gypsy lady is laughing in my head. Laughing like she does in my bad dream, when I'm tangled up on Geraldine's shelf and her curse is leaving me all alone forever.

Fallout

I don't see anybody on our street. It's like the A-bomb has already dropped and everyone has vanished but me. Like I could go up to any house I wanted and look inside and try the furniture and beds and food.

Daddy is late for work. His big white Milk Maid truck is still in our driveway. The Milk Maid girl is painted on the side. I see her happy smile clear from the corner. It's like her eyes are looking into mine. *Come on home, Cassie*, she says. *Come home.* And she watches me walk the rest of the way.

When I get to our house, I feel different. Now my heart sounds more like a drum in a cave, far off. And I'm not shaking anymore. If that noise from the plane was the A-bomb, I don't see the mushroom cloud. Maybe it hasn't happened yet.

I reach for the Milk Maid girl's perfect painted-on pigtail, her starchy white dress and the red-checked apron. The paint feels slick and hard. I'd like to pretend this truck is as strong as any bomb shelter, but I know it's not. I climb up the little step under the door and pull the handle, and the door swings out fast. I crawl inside and close it soft. The driver's seat is cold and crackles. The steering wheel is wide like a giant bowl.

Rain goes loud on the roof. It hits the windshield and trickles down. I listen a long time. I imagine standing in it and getting so wet my clothes would stick to my skin. I imagine never seeing rain again.

I sit in the one seat and pretend I'm driving, bouncing up and down. I pretend I'm turning, moving the stick that comes out of the floor. Then I remember the plane and the gypsy curse and get scared again, like I'm inside the bad dream, and I crawl behind the seat. The floor is metal with rows of bumps going everywhere. I scrunch into a ball and duck my head. I'm thinking how it will be, that if the end of the world comes now, I can jump out of the truck in time to get Mama and Nick and Boomer, and then Daddy could drive us to school to pick up Jamie.

You have to be ready; that's why people with money are building bomb shelters. Jamie says during World War II when Hitler captured the Jews, they did what he told them. They just walked right into giant incinerators and let themselves be burnt up, even when they knew what was going to happen. I can't see why they did that. I shut my eyes and think of the six of us, safe in the truck, eating ice cream until the fallout goes away.

It's warmer behind the seat. It smells like grease. I stick my head on my knees. My eyes itch from crying and my legs are heavy from running so far. I'm falling asleep.

When I wake up, the truck is moving. It hums and buckles and Daddy swears, shifting gears, then he whistles. The sound is like a bird close by, chirpy and quick. His pipe smells sweet when he lights it. I don't know what I'm going to do.

"Daddy, I have to go to the bathroom," I say when I can't wait any longer. He slams on the brakes and the truck lurches. He looks around.

"Jesus, Cassie!" he shouts when he sees me. "What the hell—" He looks at me hard, then back at the road. "What do you think you're doing?"

He waits for me to answer. I want to tell him about the end of the world and the scary plane, but not about the gypsy curse and the bad inside of my dream.

"Come on out." He points, and I crawl forward and sit where the metal floor carves a little step. "I'm taking you right back to school. You can't do things like this."

"I know," I say.

"What?"

"I know!"

He pulls over and stops the truck. He rubs his slicked-back hair down to the back of his neck. All of a sudden he looks tired. He shakes his head. Outside it's starting to hail. The hail hops up like dancing. "What's got into you?" he says.

"I'm sorry, Daddy." I push my hands hard together. My heart flips over and back. The hail dumps jacks on the roof. Like the gypsy is throwing nails. *Tell! Tell!* But I'll never tell. I want to be his little girl. I don't want him to remember I belong to Old Daddy.

"I'll be worse than late if I take you back." Daddy looks over his shoulder at the cars whooshing by.

"It's just that today might be the end of the world," I say.

"What?"

"And we don't have anyplace to go. We don't have any shelter. How come you never built a shelter?"

Daddy frowns. "Is that what's got you worried?"

I nod. "Aren't you scared?"

"Comeer, Snikelfritz," he says. His voice is softer now, and his eyes have got their little happy lights back. He lifts his arm so I can fit under, and hugs me tight. He kisses the top of my head. "There isn't going to be any end of the world. Not today," he says. "I promise."

"How do you know?" I lean into him as hard as I can. Away from the gypsy nails.

"Because I've got all this milk and all these eggs to deliver." He grabs my nose with two fingers and pulls, and when he shows me his fingers, his thumb is my nose stuck between.

I smile for him. This close I can see the tiny black whiskers starting from where he shaved. But it looks soft, too, and it won't feel scratchy until late in the day because he never forgets to shave. "But I heard a big boom," I say. "From a scary plane."

"That must have been a sonic boom," says Daddy. "It means a plane broke the sound barrier."

"But everything shook like a bomb had dropped!"

"Listen," he says, "it's just your imagination getting the best of you. It's all those stories you and Jamie make up. All that end-of-the-world stuff from TV."

I'm surprised, because I didn't know he knew about the stories.

Daddy grins. "I bet if you were to go along with me today, you'd get so busy, pretty soon the day would be over, and you'd have forgotten to be scared. Want to try it?"

"Can I?" I can't believe it. I've been waiting forever to go in the truck with him.

"Sure," Daddy says. "Why not? Go use the john at that station there, and I'll call your mom."

Underground

The hail melts to rain. I sit on the bumpy floor while Daddy drives. He drives and drives and we're driving his route, which is on a map in his head. Just before a stop he pulls his gloves on. They're brown and stiff and stay shaped like his hands when he pulls them off.

At the Milk Maid plant he backs up behind the building

where the floors are just as tall as the truck's floor, and tells me to stay inside so I won't get wet.

I sit in his seat while the men help him load the crates. The truck bounces and the crates thump and scrape. I watch for Daddy in the long side mirror until I see him. First his back and shoulders and finally the side of his face. He's standing under a roof talking in little clouds to another man.

He raises his hand and scratches his face with his carved-out glove, and then the truck door clangs and rolls shut. Daddy hops back inside.

"Thought you'd lost me?" He starts the truck and the engine roars.

I shake my head. I know he always comes back.

Downtown he jumps into the rain and tells me to watch for his signal. Then he goes around to the back of the truck and loads the dolly. When he gives the signal I get out on the rainy sidewalk. He holds my hand and we step into the place where the doors come up and an elevator goes down. Daddy pulls a handle and we sink below the ground.

"Scared?" he says when he sees my face. I look up and the doors are closing over our heads. We're in a dark, echoey place. "This is what it would be like," he says, "in a bomb shelter. Not very much fun, is it? Look there." He points and I look up at the holes in the doors, where I can still see tiny bits of sky. "Imagine not seeing the sky."

I imagine it, and I don't want a bomb shelter anymore.

We clunk bottom and Daddy unloads the dolly into a big basement freezer. When he's done he says, "Hop on the dolly," like he always does at home, and I climb on and lean back against the metal bars. Then Daddy tips me until I'm looking straight up. He pretends to let go and I fall farther back, until my stomach burns.

He won't drop me, though; he'll catch me at the last minute like he always does.

When we come up through the sidewalk again, Daddy takes me around the block and into the Milk Maid store. The people inside sit at the counter eating ice cream. The windows are steamed up from the rain. A waitress in a red-checked apron waves to us, and Daddy sits down and orders a cup of coffee.

"You look tired, honey," the waitress says to him. He's lighting his pipe. His cheeks sink in and he smiles around the stem.

"Just a little, Grace," he says. "What do you have for Cassie here? She's being a good helper today."

Grace smiles at me. "You want an ice cream, honey? Any flavor you want. Just pick." She draws a silver scoop out of a bowl of water, taps the water off, and leans into the long glass case where the ice cream rests in barrels.

"Anything but chocolate." Daddy rubs my head and winks.

"Chocolate, then," the waitress says. She digs in the barrel for a scoop. The rain swishes in when somebody opens the door. Daddy was right. Today isn't going to be the end of the world. I promise myself I won't ever let the gypsy curse work. I'm going to go on having Ellis for my daddy forever and ever, even if he isn't my real one.

Grace hands me the cone. Daddy smokes his pipe, and the chocolate tastes thick on my tongue.

Overtime

Daddy *is* tired, but I keep helping him so maybe he won't be so tired anymore. We drive to the country where houses disappear and trees and fields crowd in. The fields go flat and gray at the edge of the sky. Sometimes a barn sticks up. I sit on the metal floor and it's like the truck is moving through me, jiggling my bones and eyes and teeth.

At the egg farm the man is fat and spits on the soggy ground. "What a pretty li'l thing," he says about me. "Are you the Milk Maid?" And he gives me a dozen eggs to take home.

We eat lunch on the way back. Daddy shares his lunch from the pail. I hold the eggs on my lap and watch out the rainy glass. I think about all the things Daddy knows, about how to open up sidewalks and the back doors of stores. And how to forget about the end of the world. Back home on Diamond Street everyone is home from school. If the sun comes out they'll play in the street. But I don't care.

At the plant the boss is waving when we drive up. He steps onto the truck side and his head comes in the window. "Got a tanker needs scrubbing," he says. "You want some overtime?"

Daddy rubs his tired face. He shuts the truck off. "Okay," he says. "But I've got a hitchhiker."

The boss looks at me. "Catch her stealing eggs?"

My mouth goes dry, but Daddy laughs. "Stoop gave them to her. He thought she was the Milk Maid."

Overtime goes on until dark, which makes it seem like another day. We climb a silver ladder and look down a hole inside a milk tank. Daddy whistles into the hole and the whistling bounces around.

"Let's get to it," he says and slips down and helps me in so we can scrub the tank out.

The tank is like a tiny bomb shelter. It smells soapy and sour and the sky is the hole on top. If somebody shut that door hole we couldn't get out, and the boss might pump the tank with milk and drown us. The thought makes my bones clack.

"You took your kid down there?" the boss shouts into the hole at Daddy.

"She's all right!" Daddy yells back. "Aren't you, Cassie?"

Daddy's voice wraps around me in the tank. And then I am all right.

Milk Maid

I'm not sure how long a gypsy curse lasts, but Jamie says forever. He says the Kennedy family was cursed by a gypsy generations ago and bad things still happen to them. When I ask what bad things, he says the president of the United States has a crazy sister and a brother who died in the war. Then I'm scared all over again because what if the gypsy lady didn't just curse me. What if she cursed my whole entire family?

That's why I have a secret. The secret is a postcard from Old Daddy. I found it in the mailbox before anyone else, and I stuck it in my cigar box at home. There's a picture of Old Daddy on the front and he's wearing baggy pants and a long-sleeved shirt with a shoestring tie. His hat is pushed back on his head. His smile is squinty and his shirt sleeves fluff like he's standing in the wind.

There's a wishing well beside him. "Wish you were here!"

some big black letters say. It doesn't say where here is. Just a phone number, but I haven't told Mama or Jamie.

I don't want them to call.

"Can't I ever be adopted, Mama?"

"What are you talking about?" Mama is dotting my nose with her eyebrow pencil, making freckles.

"I want to belong to Ellis."

"You do belong to Ellis," she says. "Now hold still." I'm wearing the costume she made, and she let me do my hair in braids. But only because Daddy's boss asked me to be the Milk Maid girl for his advertisement pictures. He's trying to drum up business.

"Jamie said we have to be adopted first," I tell her.

"That kid." Mama frowns. She darkens the freckle dots and draws my mouth lipstick red. "Anyway, it doesn't matter. Ellis loves you. Look what pals you've become."

"But it's not for sure."

"Of course it's for sure. We just don't want Sikes to be too sad. Now smush your lips."

I smush my lips. "He's sad anyway. He's always saying so."

Mama laughs. "Are you ready?"

The Milk Maid dress is starchy white. It gathers at the waist where the red-checked apron ties. Mama says I look just like the girl on the truck, but the dress makes me feel like I'm somebody else, like when it's Halloween.

At the Milk Maid customers drive up to the outside counter where the boss stands. He gets the customers what they want from the glass case filled with milk, eggs, and ice cream, and they don't even have to get out of their car. The boss is wearing

Milk Maid white, too. He smiles and tips his hat when Mama pulls up. Then he slips his pencil out of the plastic pocket that fits in his real shirt pocket, and takes the next person's order.

Mama smiles back at him, but she says to me, "That *man*. I hope this advertisement thing works!" before she gets out to talk to him.

I smooth the red-checked apron. I swish my Milk Maid girl braids. There's already a scuff on my black polished shoes. I spit on my finger and try to wipe it off, but it just looks worse. Out the window the cars whoosh up next to the building.

I hope this advertisement thing works, too.

You'd never know how Mama really feels from the way she talks to the boss. When I told her what Grace said in the ice cream shop, that Daddy looks tired, Mama got cross. She talked to me like there was a mistake. "Of course he's tired," she said, "from driving that big truck all day. He should have moved into the office a long time ago."

Mama says Daddy hasn't moved into the office because he's helping make a go of things. "The boss promised him shares," she says. "But you can't eat shares. We have two families to support."

Having two families to support means Daddy sends money to Sarah, April, and Davey, but Old Daddy doesn't send money to us. When I ask why not, Mama says, "Are you kidding? You can't squeeze blood from a turnip."

I laugh, thinking of Old Daddy as a turnip, round with hairy roots. I used to think those Jacksons in his pocket made him rich, but Mama says, "No. He hardly has a pot to piss in or a window to throw it out of, even if we could find out where he's gotten to."

When there are no more cars the boss reaches under the counter and brings a camera out. Mama motions to me and I jump from the car and walk nervous across the grass. The sun pinches my eyes, but I try not to squint. Pictures look funny when you squint.

Now the boss tells me to stand under the gigantic sign where the Milk Maid girl waves and smiles. I have to wave and smile just like her.

"A regular Shirley Temple," the boss says about me.

But I'm not a regular Shirley Temple, only nobody seems to notice.

Politics

"Turn that thing off," Mama says. "It's horrible." She will not watch President Kennedy being shot over and over again on TV. He was shot while we were at school, and our principal called everyone in the cafeteria and cried when he told us. Now we have a day off to watch the funeral live.

We turn down the sound and study the pictures. It doesn't seem right to go outside and play when the president is dead. How can you act like nothing has happened? Finally Mama comes over and sits by us, but she puts her hands over her eyes when they show it. "Cover your eyes, Cass," she says. "Don't watch."

I won't cover my eyes, though. Jamie and I whisper. He feels sorriest for Jacqueline. "Imagine being right there in the car," he says. "She's the bravest woman in the world." He can't get over the way they made her stand with blood on her dress while the judge swore in Lyndon B. Johnson, the new president of the United States.

This is the part where Mama takes her hands down. Where Jacqueline stands by Johnson with blood on her dress. Mama says Jacqueline Kennedy looks like royalty. "Royalty with class," she says. "Not like the queen of England, ugly as a board fence."

They have gotten to the funeral on TV. A long line of cars and the casket riding on a horse-drawn carriage. I feel sorriest for Caroline and John-John. Caroline throws something on her father's coffin and John-John gives a brave salute.

"I told you they were cursed," says Jamie.

Murderess

This dream is different. I dream about my goldfish on the table by my bed. *I pick up the table and dump it over, and my goldfish bowl tips and falls. My goldfish swim out across the floor. They wiggle and gasp, yellow streaks with eyes, staring up at me. The water spreads to my toes, so I pull my feet away. I stand there watching them gasp, which is strange because I like them, usually. Then I get back in bed and listen as their tails hit slower and slower against the wood.*

I shut my eyes and I've got a third eye right in the middle of my forehead. No one at school knows it's there. I keep my bangs combed down so they won't see. But the teacher sees. She pulls back my hair and screams. Suddenly I'm the teacher looking at me, at my three eyes. And I can't hide them anymore.

I want a doctor to cover the third eye with skin. But the eye

112

won't cover. It sees and sees. The mess on my floor. The glass and water, my goldfish with their eye sockets soggy and white. Their sides bleached, like somebody shaved their scales off.

In the morning I get out of bed and my feet feel something wet and puffy. Cold and dead. I scream because it wasn't a dream. My goldfish have suffocated. I killed them.

"You're a murderess!" Jamie says when he runs in. He looks scared and happy, both.

"You're not a murderess," Mama says. "You were only sleep-walking again."

Fixer-Upper

Our station wagon is parked at the end of the school path. Kim Candy and I run over to the car and Daddy rolls his window down. He's wearing his work pants and jacket but has his pajama top on underneath. This is strange—Daddy never picks me up from school. And he never forgets to take his pajamas off. He must be really tired today.

"Want to keep me company?" he says.

I look at Kim. We're supposed to do our homework together. She twists a hunk of hair on her finger.

"You two have plans?" says Daddy.

"No," I say fast and jump in the car.

Now that I'm a Milk Maid girl I keep Daddy company a lot. And when we're together it's nice and my heart feels like the drawing of a heart we did in science class, with two big valves and the little hammer, thumping away right inside my chest.

"Where are we going?"

Daddy is chewing his pipe stem but he isn't smoking. He gives me a wink. "We're looking," he says, "at a good investment."

We drive out of River City and up into the mountains. The mountains have forests and old gold-rush towns. In the gold-rush towns Daddy shows me how the old-timey stores have board sidewalks and hitching posts in front. We don't stop in the towns, though; we keep going and going into the mountains.

"It's called Swede's Lodge," says Daddy. "Cassie, keep an eye out for the sign."

After a long time I find it. "There it is!" I shout and Daddy turns down a crooked road with crowding trees. He stops at a bunch of empty buildings.

"What do you think?" he says and yanks the parking brake and sighs.

Swede's Lodge is crumbly beautiful, like it used to be a rich place and just needs somebody to remember that. Behind the lodge sits a row of sagging cabins. The lodge and the cabins are tucked in a meadow with a ring of blue mountains looking down.

"Are we going to buy it?"

"We could fix her up and run her," Daddy says. "In summer you and Jamie could work in the restaurant."

It's almost dark. The sky has faded from pink to lavender blue, the trees black lace. I roll my window down so fresh air jumps at my face.

"I hear a creek," I say. "Where will we sleep?"

"Out back, in one of the cabins."

Jamie won't want to do it. We'd be too far away for him to take his dancing lessons. But I want to do it. If Daddy has a good investment he won't have to work so much and he won't be so tired anymore.

"What about Mama? What will she do?"

"She'll work here. With me." He opens his door and gets out slow. First one leg, then the other. I get out too, and button my sweater and follow.

The porch creaks. The windows have wood-framed glass squares that we look through. Inside is dusty bare stone floors and a giant fireplace. "Summer would be the busy time," Daddy says. "It snows in winter. We can learn to ski. We'll have it all to ourselves."

"I like it here." The little hammer thumps again. I think of living in a cabin, in a meadow full of snow. I think of cooking in the kitchen with Daddy. Of carrying hot steamy plates to the tables.

The best part is, if we're this far away the gypsy curse won't reach us.

Sharks

"It's getting late—where is he?" Mama's voice is cloudy. She walks around and around the house picking up toys that Nick and Boomer have left. "It's six o'clock. They were going to dock at three. He should have called by now!"

Daddy has gone on the diving-club boat in the ocean, which he's done before, but this time Mama's worried, which makes me worry, too. When it gets late she calls Janet Candy to come and wait with her. They sit at the counter drinking beer until Mama gets too nervous to sit.

"Don't get so worked up, Belle," Janet Candy says. "You want another beer?"

"He'll be home soon, I know that," Mama says, and she pops the top off the beer. "I just like to know where he is."

"Diving," says Janet Candy. "Having a good time." She pops her own beer, and the bottle cap flies up and lands on the counter, spinning. "As hard as he works, he deserves a break. They stopped to eat or something. He'll be here."

"If he'd just call." Mama is afraid of sharks. One of the divers had his leg bitten off in the Farallons. They talked about it when the diving club came to our house. That night Mama dressed up and made pizzas and we kids had to go to bed early so the club could play poker in peace.

"Call from the boat?" Janet Candy says.

"I should have gone with him." Mama frowns at Janet Candy. "For men only. Well, that's nothing to me. I can get along with men. I always do."

"You're acting like he needs a nursemaid."

"That water's so cold. He might get cramps."

"Belle, he's not going to drown."

"Don't even say it, it's bad luck."

"What, then?" Janet Candy makes one eyebrow curve like an upside-down U. I imagine the sharks grabbing Daddy's leg. The way the flesh would tear and blood ooze out, slow as ink in the water.

I get the shivers, which Jamie says means a shadow is crossing over your grave.

Mama gulps her beer. "You don't know what I know," she warns Janet Candy.

"What don't I know that you know?" Janet Candy asks.

116

But Mama won't answer, and I get the shivers again. Like when she says there's worse things than the end of the world. Like maybe she knows a gypsy curse, too.

I go down the hall to the boys' room. Jamie, Nick, and Boomer are on the bottom bunk. They've got Jamie's Indian blanket draped down to make a covered wagon, and Jamie is telling Nick and Boomer about Geronimo.

"The last great Apache," says Jamie. "But he had to surrender." He's sitting cross-legged on the bed. Sun through the blanket paints blue and yellow splotches on his chin. Nick and Boomer huddle next to him, their knees bumping. I smell their sweaty skin. Nick, who's skinny as a stalk, listens hard. Boomer's chubby little baby face is fierce.

"Geronimo only had eighteen warriors left and the army had five thousand," says Jamie. "When he surrendered, they shipped him off to Florida. Most of his people had been slaughtered. Or they died of white-man diseases."

"I'd never give up!" Boomer shouts. He pops up and waves a pretend bow and arrow.

"Sit down!" says Nick, who's always bossing him. "He isn't finished." But Boomer won't sit, so Nick punches him and they roll around on the mattress.

"Cut it out, midgets," Jamie warns, "or I'll bang your heads together." Nick and Boomer don't listen. They know Jamie would never hurt them really.

Jamie shakes his hair out. Lately he thinks he looks like Elvis Presley, the way his black curls hang down and his eyes are a perfect sad blue. He stares in the mirror a lot and then tries to practice kissing with me. Sometimes I let him and sometimes I don't.

"Is Janet still here?" he asks. Jamie loves Janet Candy. She listens to his stories.

"Daddy's late," I whisper back so Nick and Boomer won't hear.

"She's worried something might happen," Jamie says. "If it does, it will change things." He gets his faraway look, imagining Old Daddy coming back to get him.

"I wish you'd shut up about him," I say. I'm glad I haven't told him about the wishing-well card.

"I don't have to shut up."

Nick and Boomer stop wrestling to hear us fight.

"Where's Daddy?" Nick says.

"Where is he? Where is he?" I hear Mama in the kitchen like an echo.

Janet Candy pops another beer. "He's just late," she says.

The phone rings and Mama answers in her cloudy voice. "Ellis?" she says. Then, "Great!" she says, and her voice gets soft and mushy while she talks to him. "Are you—feeling all right?"

I run down the hall and Mama's holding the phone and smiling. Janet Candy is shaking her head. She peels the label off her beer and rolls her eyes when she sees me.

"I love you, too," Mama says. "No, I wasn't worried," she says. And Janet Candy snorts and takes another gulp of beer.

Jeep

The Jeep is green and looks chopped off in back. Its roof snaps on for the people who ride in front, with plastic windows that zip open or shut. The people who ride in back will be in the wind. Daddy bought it cheap from a government sale. It doesn't run, so he's been searching junkyards after work and bringing home old smelly parts of other Jeeps.

He lays them out on the floor. He works in a T-shirt even though it's almost dark, and cold. When I come riding home from my friend's I see him, his hands stained black in the creases, his long arms tanned to the T-shirt line, then white underneath. He runs one palm down his slicked-back hair, gets out a rag, and wipes the old parts down. When I park my bike he says, "What's new, Snikelfritz?" and my heart goes *boom*, because it's like he's just been waiting for me to show up.

I wasn't a good enough Milk Maid girl to drum up business. And we can't afford Swede's Lodge. But Daddy is still looking for good investments. He has the Jeep running when we get out of school, and we pack it with stuff to live outside for a whole summer, even though summer is the busiest time for the Milk Maid truck. A pick, gold pan, dredge, and tent, because the California hills are full of gold just waiting for you to find. We've got a hunting gun in case, and a stove to cook on without electricity.

Mama sits under the plastic hood holding Boomer while Daddy drives. Boomer begs to sit on my lap, but Mama tells him there's only enough room for Nick and Jamie and me to sit in back, on top of the tent and sleeping bags. We're wedged down between the spaces left in the dredge, which is a hose and pump in a plywood box, and it fills the entire Jeep back. Mama holds Boomer tight and keeps looking behind her to make sure none of the rest of us are going to fall out. We yell and wave goodbye to Sam, Kim, and Carmen Candy, standing on their porch.

My hair is cut off short for gold hunting and so is Mama's. She has a new straw hat that she pulls down low on her head. She looks out under the brim at Daddy. Whenever she does this he grins and touches her hand. "Isn't this wonderful?" she calls back to us. "This is wonderful," she says again to Daddy, as if it isn't strange at all to feel tired and take three months off work to go to the mountains.

I love riding in the Jeep. Farther and farther away from Diamond Street and the wishing-well card and the gypsy curse. The wind shouts in my ears and my eyes water. Things look more real, the trees and houses and people fastened to the ground, and we just zip on by. I can even feel the road better, how it jiggles and bumps and the Jeep sways when a big truck passes. Daddy stops to buy ice and my face feels hard, like someone's been slapping it, hoping I'll wake up.

We leave the valley and wind up into the foothills where the roads turn to dirt. The dirt shakes out behind the Jeep in clouds, and dusts the closest leaves. Big rocks stick from the mountainside into the road between so many trees beat by the sun. Birds fly at us, then flap away.

We're nowhere when Daddy sees the man with white hair. The man walks rickety out of the trees, holding a stick and patting a yellow dog. Daddy waves like he knew all along this man was coming.

"Let's see if he'll tell us his secret spot," says Daddy when he stops the Jeep. "These old-timers are finicky." His voice is low and so mysterious that even Jamie, who hardly ever listens to him, is impressed.

Daddy jumps out, and he and the old man talk under the trees where we can't hear them. While they're talking Mama pulls the canvas roof off to try and get a suntan, even though she says redheads don't tan. Her eyes look different in the sun, wiped clean. Her hair when she takes off the straw hat sticks out in all directions.

"Oooh, I feel great," she says. "I'm so glad to get away." And she fastens her eyes on Daddy.

"What's taking him so long?" Jamie whines.

"Shhh," Mama says. "That old man is a prospector. He doesn't tell just anybody where to look." She turns the rearview mirror so she can fiddle with her hair. "Oh, God," she says, "look at me." She worries over her nails, which are already split and dirty.

It's not as hot as the valley, but it's still hot. Jamie starts a story about being stuck on a slave ship heading around Cape Horn. How hot we are in the cargo hold with no water to drink and all of us shoved shoulder to shoulder. When we land in the New World we'll belong to somebody else. "Don't be so morbid, Jamie," Mama says. She jumps when a grasshopper swings up buzzing across the sky.

When Daddy comes back to the Jeep, I check to see if he looks less tired now that we're on vacation. Then I remind myself it doesn't count, he hasn't really rested yet.

"What did he tell you?" Jamie says. "Does he know where we can find gold?"

"Jamie!" Mama whispers. She looks at the white-haired man. "Well?" she says to Daddy.

Daddy winks. He starts the engine. And I know that if anybody could get the prospector to talk, it would be my dad.

When we pass the old man, I stare at him. His eyes watch me back so hard they go right through my skin. Eyes like no kind of blue I've ever seen, bluer than Jamie's eyes, bluer than the sky, bluer than cracked marbles.

"Stop," says Mama because she's thirsty. The building has wooden steps and a sidewalk like the cowboy movies on TV.

"It's just a bar," says Daddy. "What about the kids?"

"In the middle of nowhere. They can have sodas." Mama climbs out. She turns back to Daddy and her eyes are so brown in her sunburned face. She does a little cha-cha-cha and Daddy laughs. He watches her walk inside with Nick and Boomer.

The bar is cool and dim. Above our heads half a bear is charging right out of the wall. Under the bear, pool balls smack like rocks thrown together. Mama orders two beers, and she and Daddy move close to each other at our table. Jamie begs for a quarter and fidgets by the jukebox, and Daddy buys us four root beers.

"Jamie." Daddy calls him away from the jukebox. And when Jamie comes over Daddy says, "Old John has been working these hills for years and years. They're his secret. He doesn't tell just anybody what he knows."

"Did he tell you?" Jamie has his beach towel on like a cape. He flings it over one shoulder. He won't sit down. He likes to be up and moving.

"Maybe." Daddy looks excited, like he's Nick or Boomer's age, which makes me excited, too. Nobody else has a dad who takes them camping for one whole summer. Nobody else has a dad who knows how to fix up a Jeep and build a dredge and find a prospector with cracked-marble eyes.

122

Daddy slings his arm around Mama and they kiss. He chucks Nick on the chin.

"Watch!" says a man behind the bar, and he opens an orange soda and pours it in a pan. He sets the pan on the floor. We hear a thunk, and there's a deer in the open door. She looks at us and clumps over to the pan and drinks.

"Here it is." Daddy stops the Jeep but it's still running. We can look over the edge of the cliff clear to the river far below. The river is the color of a nickel and has lacy places, then slow. Where it's slow it moves in patterns that look pressed in, like the dented faces on the nickel. I hold my breath.

"Here?" Mama sounds surprised.

"Why not?"

"But it's so … there's no one around for miles."

"That's what real camping is." Daddy takes his foot off the brake and the Jeep jumps forward.

"Oh, Ellis, oh, my God!" Mama shrieks. "You're not going over this cliff? Let me out!"

"Aw, come on," he says. "We'll make it." He looks sure, sitting behind the wheel. A little wind flaps his T-shirt sleeves.

"Out!" Mama decides. She urges Nick and Jamie and me. She's got Boomer by the hand. "We'll walk," she says.

Daddy laughs.

Nick and Jamie climb out. "I'm not chicken," I say. "Can I, Daddy?"

"Come on out, Cassie," Mama says. She looks even more worried now.

I give Daddy a begging look. "Let her," he says to Mama.

Mama shakes her head no, but the Jeep's already moving,

rolling over the edge. "Hang on!" she warns, and I hear Boomer calling my name. Then the Jeep bounces and slides, going fast.

Daddy fights the wheel when it jumps away from him. His teeth shut tight together. I bounce way up and come down. In the back the tent and boxes of food and the stove and sleeping bags fly up and fall back crooked. "Whoopee!" he shouts, and we go banging and reeling all the way to the bottom.

When we stop, Daddy steals my nose and jumps out and squints at the water and sighs. I like being here first with him. He looks fine, not tired at all. The river smashes over rocks and settles into pools. The trees lean out. He takes a breath.

"Best smell in the world," he says. He pulls out the flat, round pan from behind his seat and is panning for gold when Mama and the boys come down the path.

"Look!" he says and points. I lean over the gold pan and see black sand with bits of glitter. "That's mica. Fool's gold. It means we're close."

Gold

Daddy takes moving pictures so that once we're home we can watch them together on Saturday nights. He takes us in our bathing suits getting wet and cool beside the puzzle rock, which is what we call the giant wall with all its squares of rock pressed in. He takes Mama in her new bikini, and Nick and Boomer sliding over boulders. He takes Jamie trying to climb the puzzle but falling back and trying again. Then Mama takes the camera and shoots Daddy in his wet suit, wading into the water with one arm up in goodbye.

To set up camp we roll out the tent in a big stiff square. We stick the frame together and Daddy crawls inside and lifts the tent with a pole. We lay out all our sleeping bags, six in a row, with our jackets at the top for pillows. I ask Daddy to take a picture of this, too. Nick fusses to be by Daddy, and Boomer has to be by me. Inside the tent is hot when the sun hits, and secret, like a little cave. I want night to come. I think of us sleeping in this tent every night for the whole summer, with only the outside noises and the deep dark sky.

How we'll all breathe together in this one safe place.

"Gold!" Daddy shouts over the roar of the dredge. He sits on a rock in the water and the river sucks his wet suit, his spidery legs and arms.

I race Nick over and Daddy holds the nugget up to the sun on one fingertip. "It's the real thing," he says, happy. The nugget looks duller than fool's gold, more like a tiny, shrunken potato. He admires it on his finger.

"Turn her off, will you?" He jerks his head in the direction of the dredge. Nick and I race to where the Jeep is backed up on the bank. We're laughing and we skip over the hose, strung from the dredge into the current that flows around the giant boulders. We smack into the Jeep's side before we can stop. I reach for the dredge switch and the dredge jiggers around under my hand.

It's eerie right after you flip the switch. For one awful minute the silence is deadly. The trees stand still with shock. Then the water starts to chortle again. Daddy is crouched on his rock in the sun, gleaming like a seal. Mama, Jamie, and Boomer are bending over him.

"Vial!" he calls to us, and I open the canvas door and the second smaller door on the dash. It's only a pill jar, but the pills are gone; we can count our other gold nuggets through the plastic. I let Nick carry the jar when we run back down to the bank.

Nick doesn't dare pop the lid. He hands it to Daddy, who pushes his thumb under gently, his other finger balancing the new and perfect nugget while he does this, so I know he's already weighing it in his mind, like he'll do later on our little scale at home. He moves the open jar to catch the gold and it's so beautiful when the sun hits. Then he dumps it in and caps the lid.

"We're going to be rich," Jamie says.

Daddy laughs. "New-refrigerator rich," he says, because Mama wants one.

"No, you want a boat," Mama tells him. "You should get a boat first."

I sit down and shut my eyes. Even with them shut I can see the glare of white rocks, the gleaming gold, the sun. I see a moving picture in my head like I do sometimes, not one like Daddy makes, for everybody, but a private one, just for myself. What it's like underwater. How Daddy must dive deeper than it looks from shore. Down there he sees and feels things no man has ever seen or felt, strange fish and caves and currents, light and sound playing as secret as a dream.

Rattler

The buzz sounds like a thousand crickets going and—"Don't move," says Daddy. "Rattler." We watch for rattlers everywhere, but this is the first one I've seen. I think of the little green snake-bite kit you use to cut the bite and suck out poison, tucked away in the tent.

Daddy motions me and I crawl up the rock beside him. He points to where the snake winds like a rope. Its skin is cracked and rubbery, like something both wet and dry at once. Its rattle is a skinny yellow shell.

"You really want to learn to shoot?" says Daddy. I nod and he squats beside me and holds the rifle out. "Here." I take it in my arms and his arms go around me to hold it. "She kicks," he says. His heart beats steady at my back. His breath is even. It's like I'm him and he's me and we're holding the gun together.

"Look through there," he says, and I look and see a bigger snake through the little hole. Daddy's finger moves on top of mine where it touches the trigger. "Ready?" he says, and our fingers squeeze.

The gun cracks and the snake pops up and falls down. The rifle kicks my arm and that hurts, and Daddy stands up and I'm just me again, without him. He goes over to the dead snake and lifts it up. It's as tall as he is.

"Dinner," he says.

Daddy tells everyone how I shot the snake. I feel so good when he says this, and even Jamie is surprised. I help skin it and cut it up in pieces to cook over the fire. "Got to eat what you kill," says Daddy, and spreads the skin with the rattle over a rock to dry.

"Are you kidding?" Mama says when he gives her rattle-snake meat. She won't eat it, and neither will Nick or Boomer. Daddy eats a bite and makes a big deal out of chewing and swallowing. He holds his throat like he's poisoned, and Mama says, "Stop it! Don't!" in a scaredy voice.

I take a bite, too. Rattlesnake meat lasts in your mouth like nothing else. Nick and Boomer are daring each other to eat it. I smile at Daddy over the fire. He takes another bite of rattlesnake. His face wavers, and between us sparks wiggle up and disappear into the starry sky.

It's early morning. Daddy crawls out of the tent and grabs the shovel and walks off into the woods. He walks a long way, away from the water. He stops when he hears me following.

"What are you doing here, Cass?"

"I want to come."

"You can't. Go on back." His voice doesn't sound like him.

"I can keep up."

He leans on the shovel and his face goes dark. "Go on," he says. "You can't follow me everywhere."

"But where are you going? What are you going to do?"

"Never mind." The words are pinched and sorry.

"Daddy—"

"Never mind."

I know when I've made him mad, but I just can't stop. "I'll stay behind," I beg. "I won't bother you."

"Jesus, Cassie, my stomach is killing me. I've got to use the woods!"

My face burns. How could I be so stupid? I run all the way back to the river, and sit on my favorite rock. The rock is tall and smooth and connects to other rocks that walk right out into the water. When Daddy goes under holding the dredge hose I can watch him getting gold from here. I've watched him all summer. How long he takes searching for a few nuggets, and then how glad he is when he finds one.

I stare at the rocks. Where they meet, the river has to push hard to get through. The pushing beats like the blood in my head. Dumb. Dumb. Dumb. Why do I have to be so dumb? It's not because he works too hard. Look how thin he's gotten.

The curse has found us; Daddy is sick.

Bowling

I'm between Mama and Janet Candy on the hard bench in the Nine Pins Bowling Alley. Balls roll down the bowling lanes and smash into pins. The sound of the pins knocked over is like someone smacking right inside my bones.

"So I'm leaving the son of a bitch," Janet says. "He can have the broad. She can have him." She dusts ash from her Camel into the little gold tray in her hand.

"What happened?" Mama says.

"I found her number. I called her up. I told her what I'm telling you."

Mama looks nervous and picks up Janet's Camels. She pulls one out and lights it. "This is on the Q.T.," she says to me about the cigarette. She doesn't smoke, usually.

I don't answer. If I don't say anything, I can sit here making my Coke last and listen to them talk. They talk right over the rolling balls and slamming pins and loud music, making all the noise one noise after all.

"But on your own," Mama says to Janet. "What will you do? What about money?" She plucks at her white pedal pushers and the flowered shirt she bowls in.

Janet blows smoke and squints at Mama. "I'll get a damned

job if I have to. I'll go on welfare. I don't know. The son of a bitch."

"Not be married?" Mama looks worried at Janet and puffs on her Camel. She smokes different from Janet, like someone taking tiny bites. I stare at her.

"So what about you? What's this I hear about Ellis being sick?" says Janet.

"He's not sick." Mama waves this away. "All you have to do is look at him. Does he look sick to you? We just wanted a summer off, that's all."

Janet's one eyebrow grows U-shaped, but she doesn't say anything.

Mama's ball pops up from the chute, and she leaves her Camel and sticks her fingers carefully into the holes so she won't break her nails. She stands tilted to one side, like she can hardly hold it, and bends her elbow until the ball is under her chin.

I study the Camel pack on the seat. The camel stands in a cool white desert. The package is made in layers, with a silver layer inside next to the cigarettes, and then the painted layer, and another piece of cellophane around that. The cigarettes smell like new paper in their carton. I like how neat it all is.

Janet nudges me. "Jamie says he's having an operation."

"I guess," I say. Mama just told us last night. We aren't supposed to tell anyone.

Janet sighs. "No wonder she's scared. She's so wrapped up in him. I've never seen someone so wrapped up in a man."

I watch Mama aim the bowling ball and step forward and swing. The ball thuds the floor, goes fast down the polished wood. When it hits, the pins go slamming. The machine arm floats down and picks up the pins she hasn't gotten, sweeps the rest away. She doesn't look scared; she looks like she could knock anything over she wanted to. As soon as the pins are set back, she tries again.

"Course I might stay married, too, if it was to Ellis," Janet says. "He's a nice man. Your mother found a nice man, the second time around." It makes me nervous the way she says this.

Mama writes her score on a piece of lined paper while Janet orders two beers that come in white plastic cups. The cups fit down in round holes on the sides of the benches. I drink more Coke and try to squeeze my thoughts away from the operation. Mama sips beer and checks to see if she's broken any nails. "This is good for the thighs," she says, and slaps her leg.

Music rains down from the ceiling. People leap up when they score. Janet's ball rolls out of the hole and onto the silver tray, and she picks it up and walks across the shiny floor.

"He's not sick," Mama assures me while Janet's bowling. "They're going to find that it's his appendix."

Waiting Room

Jamie and I are supposed to wait with Nick and Boomer in the waiting room so Mama can go see Daddy in his hospital room the night before his operation. We're not old enough to go in his room ourselves; you have to be fourteen. When we get there, the nurse tells Mama she can see him in a minute.

When she hears this, Mama looks upset. "Why? What's going on?" she says.

"Nothing's wrong." The nurse smiles and points to a chair.

Mama sits on the edge and her mouth twists. "He's going to be fine," she tells us. "Everything's going to be fine. Appendix is a simple operation, they do it all the time."

"But why won't the doctors say if that's what it is?" Jamie wants to know.

"When are they going to be done?" Nick asks. He scratches a mosquito bite on his skinny arm until it bleeds. Boomer crawls on my lap. He feels heavy but he's still cuddly, too.

"They can't know everything. It's just that I have a hunch. But don't you worry. He has the best doctor in the world. I wouldn't let them touch him if I didn't believe that." Mama looks so sure I think maybe she can even stop the gypsy curse.

"He doesn't act scared at all. I'd be scared," I say over Boomer's head. My breath makes his yellow hair move. "Does your appendix hurt to come out?"

"Oh, no. And they have to come out sooner or later. They're just worthless, is what they say. They make you sick in the long run. When I was little, the operation was harder. It was terrible. But they know what they're doing now. Things have changed. He's got the best doctor in the world." Mama stands up. The nurse has come from behind her counter. Mama goes down the hall toward Daddy's room. When she gets to the door we hear her say, "What are you doing? What's going on?"

Nick starts up and I hold Boomer tighter. The nurse comes over and tells us, "Don't worry, it's just a shot. Routine. To make him sleepy. I can see your mama loves him, but she's going to have to let us take care of him for a while."

"I just wish they'd tell me when they're going to do something!" we can hear Mama call. "I just wish they'd tell me!"

"So it's not his appendix?" Janet Candy asks Mama. She's helping us wallpaper the bedroom for when Daddy comes home.

Mama gives me a dirty look, but Jamie's the one who told. Then she gives Janet a sign that means not in front of me and climbs the ladder by the window. "Won't he be surprised? I had to look all over town to find this paper."

"It's okay, I can hear," I tell her. I have to hear.

"I know, honey," Mama says. "I tell you everything, don't I?" But she still won't answer Janet. She lines the paper up with the top of the wall and smooths it into place. "I found some terry cloth for the curtains, did I tell you? It's got seashells on it, with a background of blue. And terry cloth is so sensible, too. It just washes."

Below her I sweep the wallpaper brush across the paper, so the skin divers in their wet suits, their snorkels, masks, and fins, settle into place.

"So what is it, then?" Janet pastes another strip of paper.

Mama comes down the ladder. "They're not quite sure. They're going to run some tests."

Janet backs up and Mama grabs the next sheet. She starts climbing the ladder again. Janet gulps her beer that's been sitting on the windowsill next to Mama's. Her eyes find me, and I feel needle-y inside because I know what it is. It's the gypsy curse.

Janet wipes the sweat from her beer bottle. "Maybe he just needs to eat better," she says. "More protein so he won't be so tired."

"Daddy loves fish," I say. "Fish has all the protein of meat. We learned that in school."

"Fish is a good idea," Mama calls down. She rakes at her

hair, which she hasn't been able to fix, rushing back and forth from the hospital. I promise myself I'll help Mama take care of Nick and Boomer. I'll clean the house instead of going outside to play. I'll wash and fold the clothes.

I look out the window at Diamond Street, its green lawns and the trees in every yard, which have gone from sticks to being taller than me since we moved here.

"I'll start cooking more seafood," Mama says. She hangs the next piece of wallpaper and I brush it. She squeezes my shoulder. "Don't look so worried," she says. "We'll fix him up."

Mama comes off the ladder and I step back. She and Janet Candy admire how good the wall looks covered with skin divers. But the divers seem wrong to me, like they're ignoring the world, the way their hands are reaching for conch shells and their heads are wreathed in fish.

Kon-Tiki

Daddy looks pale after the hospital, and a big bandage covers his stomach. He walks around the house in his pajamas. On Saturday afternoon when he gets up he rummages in his dusty boxes again. Sarah, Davey, and April are here.

"I want you kids to choose some things," he tells us, and pulls some old pictures out. "This is me playing pony polo. This is me fishing on the bay." He sets the pictures down in a pile and picks up a book. He reads the cover. "This is a great adventure story," he says. "*Kon-Tiki*."

When Davey takes the book from Daddy my skin feels stretched.

134

"Would you read it?" Daddy asks him.

Davey shrugs. "Dunno," he says. I'd read it, but I don't say anything. That would only make Davey want it more.

"Don't take what you don't want," Daddy says, so Davey puts the book down. When he does I close my hand around it.

"I'll keep it on our shelf," I say.

Sunken Treasure

Mama walks back and forth, listening to the cars going by on Diamond Street and rubbing her charm bracelet. She says she knew she should have insisted on going with Daddy to his checkup, even if she couldn't find a babysitter for us.

It gets dark, and we feed Nick and Boomer cereal so they'll go to bed. I have to kiss Boomer four times to get him to stay put. Jamie watches TV late. He always does what he isn't supposed to do when Daddy isn't home. I hear Daddy first. His feet on the porch, heavy and scuffing. I run to the door and fling it wide. There's a chest on Daddy's shoulder; he stoops and sets it on the rug. Water dribbles out of it.

"My rug—" Mama says.

Daddy looks excited. He comes in and gives her a kiss, but not the sweeping-you-back kind. Jamie turns the TV off.

"Look," Daddy says. "I found it in the river. I had to wade the rapids; it was caught against a log. I got this deep—" He holds a hand to his neck.

Mama sucks in her breath. "But you just got out of bed this week. And your appointment—"

"I saw the doctor." He looks away, kneels by the chest. "What

135

do you think of this? It's old." He opens the clasps and the lid creaks up.

"It's wet," Mama says. "What is it? What did he say?"

"Let's see." Daddy fishes in the trunk. He pulls out some soggy newspapers. "Nineteen-oh-six," he says. "Imagine that." Some old books crumble in his hands.

"They're no good," Mama says. "It's all junk. Sweetheart?" She's so anxious she doesn't care if Jamie and I hear.

Daddy fishes some more. He pauses. His voice comes from under the trunk lid. "Cancer," he says. "He doesn't know if he got it all. If he had, I wouldn't have to worry you, Belle. But he wants to start me on this thing called radiation. It's no big deal. I can even work for Milk Maid between treatments."

His head appears and he looks sorry. He's got an old spoon in his hand. The spoon has a funny scoop on the end and scrolled flowers on the handle. He holds it out. "We'll polish it up, it could be worth something. Maybe we've found a sunken treasure."

I look at Mama. Daddy could have a monster in the trunk from the way she acts.

"Cancer?" she croaks.

Nick and Boomer have heard us. They get up and pad down the hall to Daddy, and he wraps an arm around each of them.

"Belle," he says, "don't look so scared. You'll scare the kids. It's just to make sure he gets it all."

Guilty

I want to be sick instead of Daddy, only I can't tell Mama that. She reads the thermometer and puts her cool hand on my forehead. "One hundred and one," she says. "Again! Will you be all right by yourself? Because if you aren't, I could wait." But I know she doesn't want to wait; she's got an interview for a government job.

"I'll be okay," I say. "I'll sleep."

"I don't know if you're really sick or just worried," Mama says. "But you don't need to worry. Daddy is going to be fine. Why, he had radiation yesterday and is back at work today!" Mama sticks a gardenia in her hair. The petals are pearly white and edged with brown. She smells gardenia-sweet when I shut my eyes. She doesn't realize that Daddy is cursed and it's all my fault.

"The office number is by the phone," she says. Her nylons shush across the room. The house shudders when the front door shuts. Outside, the car putters away; then it's quiet. I try holding still, but the room is spinning. I open my eyes and the walls are running like water.

I get up and go into the boys' room and lay on the bottom bunk, where the sheets feel cool. Jamie hates this room, but to me it's happy. Mama has decorated it like a circus, with fat red and white stripes down the walls. Blue drums beat on the curtains and bedspreads and our old clown-face night-light is stuck in the socket. A matching clown-face clock goes *waaah* and clicks.

My throat hurts to swallow. I want a drink, but the kitchen sounds too far away. My heartbeat whooshes in my ears. *You don't want his name I put a curse on you!*

I shut my eyes and I'm dreaming someone is in the house. Then I'm awake and the front door slams. Steps come down the hall. Twelve, says the clown clock. It's too early for anybody to be home. Except I hear him. I don't know what to do. I scrunch against the wall and bunch the blankets. I hope the bed looks empty.

It must be a burglar; I should jump out the window, only it's too high. I open the covers and look out slow. I hear man noises. I get up fast and sneak to the closet. Slide behind the door. I push way back into the toys and clothes. I feel Neal's bear and Jamie's tap shoes. I pull the clothes around me.

In Mama and Daddy's room the bedsprings creak. The man lies down and then he gets up. He's breathing in the hall. He's looking at the bedroom door, touching it.

Now the bathroom door shuts and the faucet turns on. The toilet lid slams back. These are exactly the sounds Daddy makes. But it doesn't seem like him. I crawl out of the closet to listen. I have to wait for the rushing in my head to stop. Then I go into Mama and Daddy's room. Daddy's jacket is on the bed.

I go back out and wait by the bathroom door. But I don't talk. Behind the door Daddy makes a noise like screaming from his stomach. And he hits the wall with his fist.

Snow

Now I know cancer is the gypsy lady's curse. I'm ten years old and I've only seen it snow once. Sometimes we drive into the mountains after it's already white and slide down the hills on inner tubes, but the sky is always blue as the sea. It doesn't snow here in the valley. We don't even get that much rain, just fog from the river. When it's cold and the clouds are low and still, Mama says they look like snowclouds, but nothing ever happens. The snow always passes us by.

"I thought radiation didn't hurt," I say on the way to pick Jamie up from dance class. Mama and I are alone. She's dressed up from working because she got the government job, and her hair is curled. Daddy is playing catch with Nick and Neal at home. When I said I'd stay too, Mama said, "Let the boys be together. I need you today." Lately Mama doesn't want to be by herself.

She has a beer on the Q.T., because it's illegal to drink while driving, and I have to hold it for her and watch for cops. She's drinking from a can now, and the can feels slick and cold. I shut my eyes and remember that time I saw it snow, how it came out of the sky like shredded paper.

"He feels like he has the flu, that's all. It goes away," Mama says about Daddy taking radiation. She can't keep her hands steady when she drives. I hear her moving them up and down and clicking her nails on the steering wheel. I open my eyes and she's checking her bangs in the rearview mirror.

"I wouldn't want to feel like that every week," I say. "If you ask me it's worse than the flu. When he feels sick, he goes in the bathroom and hits the wall with his fist."

Mama gets her bangs just right. She takes a look around and reaches for her beer. "Let's talk about something else, okay? Let's not talk about that."

"Okay. But he throws up."

"I know he throws up. I just can't keep talking about it!"

"Okay." *But it's my fault.*

"You get that from Ellis. That's how he is. He treats it like it's someone else. Like it's so fascinating to see all the equipment, to see how far science has come." She sounds mad.

"I don't think it's so fascinating."

Then Mama starts to cry. She hands me her beer and wipes her finger under her eyes and sniffs. "I don't know why he let them talk him into it. It just doesn't sound right. How do they know it's harmless? I mean, how do they really know? Telling him it's better than an operation."

"Anyway, he already had an operation."

"I know! I don't think they know what they're doing. Why'd they make him go through that in the first place? But he won't listen to me. *They're* the educated scientists." Mama drives faster, like she's driving over the scientists.

I look out the window at the clouds. Taking radiation is supposed to be like spending a day at the beach, like getting sun inside you, only I just think of snow. They turn the knob and it comes through you, silent, white, and shredded.

"What am I going to do?" Mama wails, scaring me. "He's my life. I'd be lost without him." She takes out her lavender handkerchief and drives one-handed and blows her nose.

"Mama?" *I'm sorry! I'm sorry I caused us to be cursed!*

"No, he's right." She sighs and puts on a fake smile. "We have to be like Ellis. He says don't panic. There's nothing to panic about. Okay. So don't you be upset either." She brakes hard and throws out her arm to keep me from hitting the dash.

At Reece's studio the door is open and music comes scratchy from the record player. "Glissade, turn, glissade, turn," Reece calls out. Jamie and the others follow, their faces hot and anxious. Reece still dances in front of the class in his black pants and shirt, an outfit Jamie has copied. When he claps his hands everybody stops, and they're quiet while he shows them what to do. He holds his arms out steady and slides across the floor, and Jamie is the only one who can follow him exactly.

"Can I talk to you?" Mama says to Reece after class. "Alone?"

I look at Jamie and start to worry. I know what she's going to do. Jamie and I wait by the open door, watching cars creep into the parking lot for the grocery store. Jamie kicks the wall with the heel of his shoe and his whole body jerks. He's always nervous after dancing, like he's still moving inside, like he's not ready to stop.

"Did he go to work today?" he asks. I shake my head. A grocery boy comes out carrying two bags, and an old lady walks past him and he follows her.

"I'd hate to lose him," we hear Reece say. "He's got a recital coming up."

"We'll put him back in when things get better," Mama says. "Right now we've got all these doctor bills and we just can't—"

Jamie's foot stops moving. He looks like he might break.

"Let him stay until the recital," says Reece. "No charge. He's worked so hard. He's earned that much."

Jamie's foot starts moving again; he tucks his hands under his arms, and hunches.

Jamie won't talk on the way home. He sits in the back seat, which he never wants to do, and stares out the window. Mama watches him in the rearview looking worried, and her eyes want me to help. "Now, when we get home, Jamie's got to mow the yard. He's got to do it before Ellis has to ask, okay?" she says to me as if Jamie can't hear.

We pass the mall, which covers the entire field now where the white horse used to run. Beyond that a line of trees grows along the river.

"Cassie—" Mama warns. "Is he listening to me?"

Writing to Old Daddy

"I don't have time," Jamie tells me about the lawn. "I have to write a letter. You kids get out of here." We're in the boys' bedroom with the circus stripes, and Jamie's bulletin board looks out of place, covered with the dreamy pictures he draws of movie stars.

Nick ignores him when he says get out, and goes on playing with our old Lincoln Logs. He's got plastic sheep and horses corralled in plastic fences around his fort.

"I mean it," Jamie says, "all of you."

"Mama said you have to do it," I say.

"Mama said," Jamie mimics. "If you're so worried, why don't you do it for me? You're the helpful one."

"If you don't, Daddy will get mad."

"I don't care. It doesn't matter to me. I'm not going to be here that long."

"Where are you going to be?"

"Places. Now get going. Everybody." He glares at Nick and Boomer.

"It's our room, too," says Nick.

"Did he say he was coming? Did you find him?" I get shaky

thinking Jamie might find Old Daddy even without the wishing-well card with his phone number.

"None of your business," he says.

"It is too."

"Find who?" Nick says. He doesn't remember that Jamie and I have another father. I don't explain it to him.

"You don't want to see him, so why do you care?" Jamie says to me.

"Who?" Nick says again.

Jamie sits down at his desk. He looks at his pictures of Marilyn Monroe.

"Do you want me to do your mowing, Jamie?" I say. "I will." Now I get shaky because I have kept the wishing-well card a secret.

"No."

"I will. Just this once." Jamie doesn't look at me. He's starting to write his letter.

Daddy wants to know how come I'm doing Jamie's job. He's in the backyard putting up a basketball hoop for Nick and Boomer, even though they're too short for basketball. "You've got to have something to reach for," Daddy says and pours cement into the hole he's dug. He stands the post with the hoop on it. He checks it with his level. Daddy feels better today—he always feels better a few days after he gets radiation and throws up.

Nick and Boomer come outside, excited to watch. I tell Daddy I traded with Jamie and he's going to do my dinner dishes.

"I'm sorry about his dancing," Daddy says. "I'm sorry your mom has to work. I'm not going to let things stay this way for long." He looks around the yard. "We need something here.

Something more. A garden, I think, and some fruit trees." He's sweating, and he wipes his forehead with his handkerchief. "Home-grown vegetables and fruit are good for you. Better than store-bought."

"I'll help water the garden," I say. I don't want things this way for long, either.

Daddy smiles and grabs the basketball from Boomer. He throws it high in the air and it goes sailing through the net.

"When this is over we'll build our boat and go sailing around the world," he says. "You reading *Kon-Tiki*?"

I nod. "What about school?"

"We'll get you kids out of school. You can study from a book."

Jamie won't want to do it. It's the same problem he would've had with Swede's Lodge. But I'd go in a minute.

"You know, I'm luckier than most," Daddy says to me. He looks toward the kitchen window, where we can hear Mama stacking dishes. "We live in an age when this stuff can be cured." He puts his arms around Nick and shows him how to make a shot. Nick listens while he says, "Hold here, spread your hands, shoot!" But then Nick throws the ball straight up over his head.

Being Good

The government work gives Mama backaches. Her high heels make her feet hurt. "Brush," she says when she gets home. She kicks off her shoes and stretches on the couch and Jamie and I fight over the plastic brush.

"It's my turn!" Jamie says, yanking it away.

"Let her, Jamie," Mama says when I shout. "You rub my feet." So Jamie sits at Mama's feet, but I feel his eyes hot on me.

Mama's toes look bunched up in her stockings. The paint on her toenails is candy apple red. We know where her feet hurt, right in the curve that her high heels make.

"Oooh," she says when Jamie tickles. She leans her head back. She has so much hair thick to her shoulders and the big curls are sprayed in place. I sweep the brush down and her hair is stiff at first—I can smell the spray. Then I brush it soft. Mama says how nice the brush feels. She frowns, snaps her earrings off, then rubs the dents in her ears.

Ever since Mama got the government job, Jamie and I have to walk to a sitter's house after school. Her name is Mrs. Klieg and she has three boys. Nick and Boomer are already there. She makes us all play outside. Jamie complains that he's not going to go to her house at all. He doesn't see why Mama has to work when Daddy can drive the Milk Maid truck on his good days.

Jamie has an F on his report card. He shows it to me at the bike rack after school. "Swear you won't tell," he says.

But I don't see how they won't know. "They have to sign it, Jamie," I say.

"You don't know anything," Jamie says. He doesn't ask to see my report card, but I tell him what I got anyway. "A's are no big deal," he says. He yanks his bike from the rack. "You don't need A's to dance." He doesn't walk his bike down the path, which is a rule from the one-armed principal. He rides instead.

A whistle blows, but Jamie ignores it.

"But if you flunk they'll keep you in school forever!" I shout. I run beside my bike trying to catch up to him.

Jamie looks over his shoulder at me. "Anyway, I'm not going to *her* house today," he shouts back.

"You have to! We're supposed to go to the sitter's unless Daddy is home!"

Jamie stops at the end of the path. "Not me," he says when I catch up. "I'm going home to practice before anyone gets there." He's cleared a spot in the garage, and he plugs his phonograph in above the washer to dance.

"Then I won't go if you're not."

"Yes, you will." He jumps back on his bike and pushes off. He grips the handlebars and his shoulders yank up and he rides away fast down the street.

I bike slowly to Mrs. Klieg's. She has a number-two house that's nicer than ours. I knock on her door and she answers and Nick and Boomer run up and grab my hands and pull.

Mrs. Klieg is so big her front buttons won't close right. "Where's Jamie?" she says. I look in the peek holes between her buttons and shrug.

Mrs. Klieg calls Mama at work. I hear her on the phone. I want to talk to Mama, but no one is supposed to call except in an emergency.

I hate Mrs. Klieg's. There's no place to be. There's no one my age to play with, and her living room has a new flowered couch so kids can't sit. I stay on her kitchen stool and read *Kon-Tiki*. Thor Heyerdahl and his crew made a balsa raft and sailed it from Peru to Polynesia to prove it could be done. Thor Heyerdahl reminds me of Daddy.

I watch *Popeye* and *Mr. Ed* with Nick and Boomer. I help

146

Mrs. Klieg make dinner by cutting up carrots, cabbage, and celery, but we'll have to leave before we can eat any. I'm hungry, but Mrs. Klieg doesn't believe in snacking before dinner. I'm thinking about Jamie at home practicing his dance.

Jamie's dancing Pinocchio in his recital, which is the lead. Pinocchio's nose grows when he lies, and he can't be human until he listens to his conscience. Sometimes I feel as wooden as Pinocchio. And that having a terrible secret is even worse than telling a lie. Jamie thinks I'm being smart-alecky getting A's. He doesn't know how I really feel. How hard it is to be good so maybe I can change things.

Mud and Tiger's Milk

In the kitchen the moves Daddy makes are hard and quick with the bowls and knives and spoons. He opens the book by Adelle Davis telling you how to eat the right foods, and props it against the mixing bowl. "I'm going to invent a famous vegetarian spaghetti sauce," he says. He chops parsley and the knife goes so fast the blade is four blades moving.

He has the milk shake mixer going. It screeches when he takes the silver cup off. The silver is shiny with sweat and cold in my hands when he gives me a drink. "What is it?"

"Tiger's milk."

I laugh. "How do you milk a tiger?"

"Do you like it?"

"I'm not sure."

"It's healthy. Better than milk. There's more vitamins."

Since he's sick he worries about vitamins a lot. He says he

needs more energy. He eats funny things called brewer's yeast and sea kelp. And just like when we had rattlesnake meat, Jamie, Nick, and Boomer hold their noses and won't try it. I'm the only one who will.

"Yuck," says Jamie when he comes in from school, "what is this stuff?"

"You forgot to take the garbage out," says Daddy. "You forgot to smash the cans."

"I have to practice for my recital."

"You can practice after." Daddy shakes his head and Jamie folds his arms across his chest. Daddy looks tired the way he rubs his slicked-back hair down to the back of his neck. I set the tiger's milk down.

"But I hate smashing those cans," Jamie whines.

"Don't talk back," Daddy warns, and Jamie drags the garbage outside looking mad.

"I can't stand it when he's home," Jamie says when I follow him out. "He's always telling me what to do. He doesn't care about my recital."

"You'd better do what he says," I tell Jamie. "He doesn't feel good again."

"Yeah, do what he says, like Miss Goody Two-Shoes." He smirks at me.

"I'm *not* a goody two-shoes! Quit saying that!"

"Goody, goody, goody." The sledgehammer hits the concrete loud and the cans crumple. Jamie tosses them aside.

I glare at him. He stops smashing cans. By the garbage can there's a side garden, then a sidewalk and a strip of grass, and then the neighbor's grass and sidewalk and garden, like a matching set. There aren't any plants in the gardens, only mud.

He pulls off his shoes and walks into it and the mud squishes around his toes. A rotten smell comes up.

He picks up a glob of mud and eyes me.

"Don't," I say. "I mean it."

He lifts his arm and I duck behind the garbage can. He rattles the can and I look up and he mashes smelly mud in my hair. I run over to the neighbor's side of the grass and he pelts me. I duck and the mud splatters the neighbor's wall.

A fist has grabbed my throat. "Old Daddy is never coming back!" I yell. "And I'm glad!" *I'm glad I fixed it!*

Jamie's face turns red. "Shut up," he says.

"He's nothing but a drunk!"

"He's our dad," Jamie says, "and Ellis isn't!"

"Well, I hate him." *He let the gypsy lady curse us!*

We stare at each other. Jamie lets go with more mud. The neighbor's wall is wide and pink, pale pink, with little bumps everywhere under the paint. The mud sticks like tar. Jamie picks up another handful and hits it again.

"You're really going to get it this time," I say.

"But you never do." He picks up another glob. Throws. Over and over until there's black all over the neighbor's pink house.

Burn Barrel

"What's wrong with that kid?" Daddy shouts to Mama. "Why does he do these things?" He looks wobbly, standing by the dining table in his pants and pajama top. Mama stays in the kitchen, letting the water run. She says something I can't hear over the rushing. But our house is so open I can hear and see everything else. Jamie's in his room, hollering because Daddy licked him with the belt. In the living room Nick and Boomer stop bouncing on the couch and sit down, trying to act like they're being good. They get a lot of spankings but never with a belt.

"He's going to have to go over there and try to scrub that mud off," Daddy says. "We'll probably have to pay them for new paint." Neither Mama nor Daddy will shut the water off. It's hot water, and steam comes up and hits the window and makes a whitish cloud.

Jamie's still hollering.

"If you don't quiet down I'll give you something to cry about," Daddy calls to him. He heads down the hall and I start to follow.

"Stay here, Cass," Mama warns.

"He'll hit him again."

Mama shakes her head. "He doesn't feel well. Jamie pushes his buttons."

But I have to follow. I run after Daddy. I catch up just as he's opening the bedroom door. Jamie huddles on his top bunk. He's holding his Indian blanket and his thumb is stuck in his mouth. No one but me knows he still does this.

"Give that to me," Daddy says, surprised. "You're too big for that."

Jamie looks stubborn and shakes his head.

"I mean it. You're twelve years old." Daddy's face gets red.

Jamie tries to scoot way back in the corner where Daddy can't reach him, but Daddy is too tall. He grabs the blanket anyway. Jamie won't let go. Daddy pulls and Jamie pulls and for a minute they look so funny I want to laugh. Then Daddy reaches out and grabs Jamie's hands and forces his fingers off the blanket, one at a time. Jamie starts to scream.

Daddy has the blanket now. He stomps out the door and past me down the hall, and Jamie yells, "I hate you! You're not my father! I wish you were dead!"

I run into my room and slam the door. I curl on the floor and cover my ears, push under the bed where it's cool and dark. I still hear Jamie. The sound comes through my closed door and past my ears into my skin, where it sits in my stomach like a stone. *I hate you. I wish you were dead.*

I hear Mama go in the bedroom and talk to Jamie. I hear Daddy slamming out the back door. I get up and run out after him. He's stuffing the Indian blanket in the burn barrel. My bones get light, like they're stretching and falling apart. Jamie has slept with this blanket forever. I look back at his high window and I can see his face, pinched up like an old man's face, watching. Daddy settles the grate and sprinkles fluid to make the fire burn.

"No!" I shout and he turns around and sees me. I'm scared of his mad red look, but I scream at him anyway. "He loves that blanket! Don't burn it up!"

Daddy sighs and steps away from the barrel when the blanket starts to smoke.

That makes me hate him as much as Jamie does. I run for the hose and push at Daddy and squirt the barrel like I'm crazy.

"Stop it, Cass!" Daddy yanks the hose away.

I yank it back.

"Give me that hose!" Daddy yells.

"I did it! I did it! I did it!" I yell back. *I made the gypsy mad and hid the postcard and cursed us all.* "I made you sick! I wasn't supposed to love you best! But *you* are supposed to be our dad forever and ever!"

Black smoke and flames rush up from the barrel. It's too late. I can't put the fire out. And Daddy stares at me until the mad red cracks from his face and a tear leaks down.

Logan

"Cassie," Daddy says. "My getting sick is *not* your fault."

We're sitting on my bed, on the pink polka-dot spread Mama bought me. Daddy has his arm around me. I feel shuddery and I smell like blanket soot.

"You hear me?" Daddy says.

"But—"

"No buts," he says.

The polka dots are raised white bumps. I rub my hand across them.

"Do you know how I got cancer?"

I hate that word. I shake my head.

"From my dad." Daddy pulls my chin up. "I probably inherited it."

I feel surprised. Daddy never talks about his father. He only talks about Grandma. Whenever we visit her house by the ocean she's always there alone. Daddy keeps holding my chin so I have to look at him. His face isn't red or mad or cracked anymore. It's Daddy's face again.

"I don't know anything about your dad," I say. "What's his name?"

"Logan. His name was Logan."

152

"He'd sort of be my granddad."

"Well, I never really knew him much." Daddy squeezes my chin.

"Why not? Where is he?"

For a minute Daddy looks like Thor Heyerdahl, staring out across the Pacific Ocean. Then he says, "He died. But I'm not going to. They have better medicine now. For things like this. So you keep this chin up." He lets me go.

"I'm sorry, Daddy," I say. "I got you wet with the hose."

He laughs. "You're lucky I didn't whack you." And he grabs my nose and opens his hand and sends our old joke into the air.

Part 3

"Laugh and the world laughs with you;
weep and you weep alone."

—*Mom*

Vacation

The summer I turn eleven, Ellis loads up the car and drives us all to Mexico.

The beach stretches empty warm and blue and Jamie is buried up to his neck in sand. Nick and Boomer are digging holes. Ellis suits up to dive. Even though the water is warm, he still gets cold. He opens his wet suit and pours powder down the legs and arms, then steps inside. The wet suit squeaks against his skin.

"Take his picture, Mom," I say and she aims the movie camera. She takes his picture walking backward into the waves, grinning, with his face mask sucked to his face. Then he kicks out past the waves holding the inner-tube boat he made, with plywood lashed to make a seat, and a red flag waving on top.

Ellis kicks out and out until he's just a little dark spot. He dives down and comes up and his head is as wet black as a seal's. He plops something in the little boat. A lobster.

I want to be out there with him. I walk down to the waves and stick my feet in. Behind me Nick and Boomer chase each other around the sand. On the surface Ellis's inner tube bobs and ducks. I wade out to my waist. I stand in the water's slap. The air smells so clean it hurts. I wade to my shoulders and wait. A big wave comes and I dive through it, go farther out, swimming.

I turn and look at the sky. I feel another wave building. Its big shoulder rolls up and then goes rushing fast. I count to seven like Ellis taught me, to get the biggest one. When it comes I turn and start swimming fast. But it's bigger than I thought. So big and so fast I can't stay on top. I can't see the sky anymore. I shut my eyes and open them and they sting with salt.

I'm underwater.

I'm rushing backward and down and hit something hard and sand stuffs my mouth. My cheek burns. When I hit I can't hold my breath and I suck in water. I can't find the air. I kick out for the surface, but it's not there. My chest aches enough to burst. The blue is gone, replaced with black and bits of silver star. I'm sucked out to sea and I'm going to die.

Then I'm moving in again, going up. My feet are scraping sand. I kick bottom and I'm in the little waves, pulling air. I cough and water comes rushing out. I crawl out of the waves.

Everybody is just like they were. Mom and Nick and Boomer, Jamie in the sand buried up to his neck. Ellis is chugging out of the surf. He's got six lobsters in the boat. He holds one up and wiggles it in the air at Mom so she shrieks and runs away.

Later we gather wood for a fire, and Mom puts the big pot over the flames. Ellis dumps the lobsters in and they make tiny screaming noises, dying. When they're cooked the meat is white and good, better than rattlesnake. And we eat them sitting in the sand, dipping them into melted butter so the butter runs down our fingers and wrists.

My cheek feels scraped where it hit the sand, but nobody realizes. Nobody knows how scared I was. Or that I finally understand. Cancer is not a gypsy curse. It's a huge smashing wave. It catches you and drags you out. And anybody can be spit back up, and anybody can drown.

Vending Route

At the gas station our cigarette and candy machines sit behind streaked glass in Harv's dusty office. Harv is pumping gas; he sees Ellis and juts his hand in the air. Ellis waves and opens the cigarette machine with a key and counts out the packages that are left. Jamie and I open our new used station wagon and stack boxes from the back onto the dolly we kept from the Milk Maid.

Ellis finally found an investment and quit driving the Milk Maid truck. He bought a vending route that has machines all over town. He's showing us the route. The car is parked in the shade but it's still hot.

Harv walks by, whistling. "Out helpin' the old man, huh?" he says to Jamie. Jamie glares. He doesn't like Ellis's new investment. He thinks it's too much work.

When we're loaded, Harv steps back so we can wheel the dolly past him. Inside, we cut the cigarette cartons open with a razor blade and refill the low stacks. The packages fit neat and shiny in their wrappers, like stiff pillows. They slide into the stacks so the ends show. Ellis pulls out the change box and dumps it in a canvas moneybag. We'll count the money at home. Harv is at the door, watching.

"It's a good machine. A good location you got here," Harv says. He scratches his belly. His blue shirt with the sewed-on name is buttoned wrong.

Ellis draws the bag shut. The dollar-bill sign on its front bulges. "Wish they were all this good," he says. He leans against the machine and his face is pale.

"Hey, man, you okay?"

"No problem, just a minute." Ellis rubs his forehead with the heel of his hand. It's broiling in the little office. It smells greasy. I step closer to him.

Harv looks embarrassed. He slaps Ellis on the back and says, "Hang in there, man." Then he turns away.

"Let's go." Ellis lifts the moneybag, and it bumps against his knee when we walk back to the station wagon and climb in.

Hot air pushes in from the open windows. The radio announcer says it's going for one hundred and nine degrees. Ellis sweats driving. Jamie sits up front with him, and I'm on the folded-down seat next to the boxes of gum and candy and cigarettes. We have more boxes stacked on the floor of our garage. There's no place for Ellis's old carpentry tools, which are all shoved to one side to make room for a pinball game and a candy machine that need fixing. Ellis is worried about having them out of commission, since they could be making us money. He's mad at Jamie for stealing Hershey and Mounds bars from the boxes. He says Jamie's eating all our profit. I hold my breath but they don't fight like usual.

"It's not hard, Jamie," Ellis says when we hit the freeway for the west side. "All you have to do is memorize the route, bring the supplies you need, and remember which spots need service when. Mom can drive you." He says this as if, any minute, he won't be here to help us. I look out at River City slamming by. Diamond Street is full of plants and trees, but here it's so many cars and blank-eyed buildings, I can't even see the river.

"You have to get a feel for it," Ellis says. "It can make you money. I know it can."

Jamie's quiet. Ellis stops talking and the air inside the car is thick and slow as mud. I almost wish Jamie would pick a fight with him after all, so things would seem more normal. Ellis mops at his dripping forehead with a white handkerchief, and Jamie and I look at each other across the back of the seat.

Blue Book Coins

At night we count the mounds of nickels, dimes, and quarters from the vending machines. Then we stack and roll them for the bank. My hands smell like metal and my eyes are tired from searching for Indian Head nickels, Liberty dimes, and quarters with rare mint dates. When we find a rare coin we stick it in the blue book. The blue book is a cardboard folder with three-way folds, which open to rows of dated holes.

Most of the good coins we find aren't that valuable. They're too thumbed over, the tiny words and numbers worn by a river of human hands, but we collect them anyway. It's different from when we hunted for gold, but it's the same, too. Maybe someday we'll find The One. The one that will make us rich.

"The main thing is the house," Ellis tells me when I give him the rolled-up coins. "You've got to keep up with the payments."

"What payments? I thought this house was ours."

"Ours and the bank's," says Ellis. "We have a loan." He explains to me how this works. How you pay every month until you pay off the loan. And then the house is really yours.

"Until then, you can't miss more than two months," says Ellis. "Or the bank can take your house back."

Sleepwalking Again

I've changed, but Mom has changed more. Ellis has been cooking because she's stopped doing it. If he doesn't feel good we eat boxed things for dinner that Jamie and I bring back on our bikes from the store. We eat sandwiches and cereal, but Mom doesn't even eat that. She just chews peanuts and drinks Coke, or beer when Ellis isn't watching. And she's been coming into my bedroom at night.

"Just to check," she says, her hands doing nervous things. She lies down beside me and her voice sounds distant, like she's talking to herself, like I'm not even here. She's gotten almost as thin as Ellis.

"I'm writing to the Mayo Clinic," she whispers. "They're experts on this. Not like these fools here." Mom will not say the word *cancer* out loud. "If you ask my opinion, they gave him something with that radiation," she says. "I don't think he was even sick before they opened him up. And I'm not going to rest until he has the best doctors in the world. Do you know what you just did?"

"What?" Her new voice worries me. A voice like Nick or Boomer when they're caught doing something bad and are trying to cover it up. A voice that begs, "Don't hurt me," which doesn't seem right, since Mom hasn't thought much about herself in all this time, she's just thought about getting Ellis well. But then she's never actually said he was sick before, either.

"You've been walking in your sleep again," Mom says. "You came into our room and stood there. Don't you remember?"

"No." I haven't walked in my sleep since I dumped over my goldfish bowl that time.

"You asked me if everything was all right."

"I did? What's the Mayo Clinic?"

"A really good place. The best in the world for curing stuff like this. That's why I want you to stop worrying. You worry too much. Everything's going to be fine." She snuggles close as if she never worries at all, and I can smell her Jean Naté After Bath Splash and her Aqua Net hairspray and the other smells that are her.

When the Mayo Clinic writes back, they say Mom should trust our doctors, that what they're doing for Ellis is nothing more than he'd get at the clinic itself. "They're in cahoots," she decides. "All these doctors are. They know each other, see. They go to the same schools. They have the same rich friends. You can't really expect them to admit it when one of their own has done something wrong." She leans close to show me the letter, and makes little digging motions at the page with her fingernails.

"Don't you feel good, Mom?" I say. "Maybe you should go see Janet for a while."

"I was just over there." She visits Janet a lot after work, especially if Ellis is resting in bed with the door shut. "Don't tell anyone that it's the doctors who've made Ellis sick," she goes on. "You can't go around blabbing things until you're sure. Until you have proof positive. Think how he would feel!"

Ellis notices it too, the way Mom's gotten. He says working the government job leaves her tired, that she'll be okay once the vending route catches hold. He says it's because she has to get up early and fight the traffic and sit at a desk all day. But he's going to work out something better.

"Don't be silly," Mom tells him. "I have the energy of a dozen people." And it's true she's always busy, always "on the go" like she says she wants to be. Even when she's home she's moving around, jumping up to get things for Ellis or cleaning out the drawers and closets. But it's different.

She never sews our clothes or goes bowling like she used to. Sometimes she doesn't even set her hair, and wears it tied up in a scarf. On Sundays, she gets out of driving us to Sunday school by giving us money to ride our bikes to Winchell's, and then we bring the doughnuts home and eat them, laughing at the boring preachers on TV.

The Old Man

Ellis stands next to his overnight bag in the hospital lobby. He's having another operation. We have to say goodbye out here because in this hospital kids under fourteen aren't even allowed upstairs. His eyes look bright and far away. I helped him pack. He's got his shaving kit inside, his striped pajamas, the brown slippers with the low sides, and even though smoking isn't allowed, his best stitched leather pipe. He hugs Nick and Boomer and kisses Grandma, who's come to help. He holds Jamie's shoulders and tells him to be good. When he gets to me he grabs my nose with his right fist and brings his left hand down with a loud whack. He shows me his thumb stuck between his fingers. "Got your nose," he laughs, although I'm too big for this now.

"You'll help your mom and Grandma?"

"I'll help."

"Good." He smiles at me and I feel older than eleven the way he counts on me, but I don't want him to go.

Ellis has his operation while we wait in the plastic chairs. A nun wearing a black habit sits at the front desk. A cross with Jesus being tortured hangs behind her head.

Mom looks at her watch and checks her nails and pokes her hair a hundred times. She walks back and forth and back and forth across the shiny floor. Every time someone steps on the pad that opens the electronic doors, she jumps. She's gotten more and more nervous about hospitals. "I hate these places," she keeps saying. "I hate these places."

Jamie wanders into the gift shop down the hall and starts talking to the saleslady. Something he says makes the saleslady smile.

"If they hurt my daddy I'm going to get a bomb and explode them all," declares Nick, glaring at the nun. He's sitting by Grandma and craning to see the wall TV. Grandma always looks old-fashioned. She dresses in Crayola colors, a purple dress and salmon sweater. Her black shoes hit clunky on the floor. She hugs Nick against her chest and her eyes get wet. Nick wrestles free. There are grass stains on the split-open knees of his pants. His shirt is stained with Kool-Aid.

"You shouldn't let him talk like that," I tell Mom. "He talks about guns and bombs too much." Nick makes a face at me.

"Never mind," Mom says.

"Bombs kill. They tear off arms and legs. They—"

"You play army with the boys all the time," Mom interrupts. "What's the matter with you?"

Boomer's sitting next to me. I try to smooth his cowlick that no amount of water will straighten. "I used to play army. I don't anymore. Now I know about real war. I know the truth."

"Don't argue." Mom stretches her fingers and checks her nails again. She rummages in her purse, but she can't find whatever it is that's lost in there. Her face looks blank and startled, trying not to think about Ellis. Nick starts watching *My Favorite Martian*, and his thin cheeks go pale from the light of the screen.

The doctor comes out in his green baggy pants when *My Favorite Martian* is over. Grandma and Mom rush up to talk to him. Grandma's quiet but Mom begs, "What is it? What's happened?" in her most scared voice.

"He's in recovery. He did just fine." The doctor pats her arm like she might bite.

"Already?" Mom clutches Grandma's hand. I stand up and walk over. The doctor notices me.

"We'll go over things in private," he says.

Ellis has to stay in the hospital for two weeks. I bug Mom to let me see him until she finally agrees. "That rule isn't fair anyway," she says, making me happy that she sides with me. She looks angry saying it. She tells me she's decided all doctors are imbeciles, although she never says this when she talks to them in person. At the last minute Boomer begs to come with me, so we go to the hospital together. Mom sneaks us upstairs and tells us to sit in some chairs in the corridor while she goes down the hall to Ellis's room.

It's creepy upstairs. Old-food smells and disinfectant. A janitor clangs a mop into a bucket and leaves it by the elevator doors. Boomer fidgets and presses against me. He asks how long we'll have to wait.

"Not long," I say. "Sit still. You wanted to come." So he slumps down in his seat and kicks the chair rung. I try not to look into the open room doors. If I sit just so, bent forward a little, my body rocks on its own. It's like a pulse, or a big clock, ticking. I feel the ticking and stare at the wall opposite me. Then I turn and look down the hall where the window's slow with sun. An old man is coming toward me. His hospital gown hangs around his shoulders and down in front. He takes little shuffling steps. He's leaning on a cane. I look down at Boomer's bent head. I can smell the mop bucket by the elevator; it smells like too much bubble gum.

I decide not to look at the old man when he walks by. I keep watching Boomer's head. It seems to last forever, listening to him coming. But he doesn't pass by. He stops right in front of us. I look up and it's Ellis, standing there.

"Bored?" He smiles and I start to shake.

"Daddy," Boomer says.

"Hey, Buddy." Ellis rubs Boomer's head.

"Are you getting better?"

"They just had some repairs to make. But I'll be home in two days. How about that?" He lifts my hand and puts it between his on top of the cane, and I think of that game where you take turns sliding your hands out to be the one on top. "Got to go lie down again, okay? Thanks for coming to see me, you two."

He turns around and shuffles down the hall. Mom hurries out of the room to get him and grips his hand like he's a baby. The worst thing is that the back of his gown is open. At home she won't even let him come out of the bathroom in his underwear. "Ellis, the kids," she always says. But today he's not got anything on underneath. I can see everything, and the nurses and the other patients can see everything, too.

"Come on." I jump up and yank on Boomer's arm. "Let's get out of here."

"Ouch," Boomer yelps, surprised. "Let go."

I hold on tighter. I drag him to the elevator, stand next to the mop bucket, and push both buttons at once. When the doors open I kick the mop bucket hard, and the dirty water sloshes out and pools on the linoleum. I don't care. I kick it again and send the bucket skating down the hall. I drag Boomer inside. He's quiet now. A nurse is running toward us when the elevator doors close us in. I'm scared the wave is not going to spit Ellis out.

When Ellis comes home, he calls to Nick and Boomer when they come slamming in from school. They're shy running to his room, as if when he's lying down they forget who he is. They show their schoolwork with grubby hands, and Ellis takes their papers and studies them.

"How was it today?" he says and Nick and Boomer squirm and shuffle their feet. They punch each other in the arm. Neither of them can ever stand still.

Ellis asks Nick about long addition, which he's good at. He asks Boomer how his reading is coming along. Then he spreads out the Chinese checkers and Nick is a bad sport if he loses, so Boomer teases him to make him mad.

Driving Around

"Mom, he doesn't look so good."

"What?" Mom's eyes flick from me to the road. It's different driving with her than with Ellis. She moves so quick, in and out of stores, jumping into the car and turning the key, backing out of parking spaces. She lets me play my music and thumps her hand on the wheel to the beat. She's got another beer between her legs, on the Q.T. again, and the rest of the six-pack is on the floor by my feet. Whenever we pass a cop she covers the top so he won't see the can's reflection in the windshield. The sicker Ellis gets, the crazier Mom gets. Our next stop is the cleaners, the one that takes a big load by weight. Our dirty clothes are piled up in back.

"Yesterday," I say, "he said he couldn't work the machines."

"Oh, well, he's so tired, that's all. He's worn down. Who wouldn't be discouraged?" She glances at herself in the rear-view mirror. She purses her lips. "Hand me my lipstick, will you? I get so dry. Just in that little top pocket, you know." Mom does not like me to rummage in her purse.

I find the lipstick and she draws it on, one hand still on the wheel, the beer safe between her legs. "See, that's why we got the machines. They're something he can work at and be his own boss. When he doesn't feel like getting up, he doesn't have to."

"He's brave, isn't he? I mean he doesn't ever say how much it hurts."

"Very brave. You should hear the guys from the diving club, they're amazed at the way he is. He just never complains. They can hardly believe it." She hands me the lipstick tube. Her lips gleam bright red. Her eyes are teary. I breathe harder, thinking with her how brave Ellis is.

Mom brakes suddenly for a light and throws her arm out to keep me from hitting the dash. I push her hand away. I'm old enough to catch myself.

"What if he doesn't feel like working the machines at all?" I say. "Then what?"

"Well, we've been talking. I might quit the office and take over. And Moss has offered to help. You know Moss, from the club? He's going to help us on that. Just until Daddy gets better." I think of Moss with his watery blue eyes and fat belly.

"Daddy wants Jamie to work with him on the machines after school, but Jamie doesn't want to."

Mom glances around and takes a fast gulp of beer. "Jamie wants to help, don't kid yourself. He's miserable about all this." She likes to pretend that Ellis and Jamie have always gotten along perfectly.

"I'll do it," I say. "Tell Daddy to let me do it. I know how."

"Oh, honey."

"Don't say I'm a girl!" I shout at her. "I can do it."

She looks surprised. "All right," she says. "All right."

"Jamie can watch the boys," I say. I'm still mad. I slap the dash. "Have you heard from Mexico yet?" I ask. "Have you got a letter?" After Mom gave up on the Mayo Clinic, she started writing to Mexico. She says the cure in Mexico is the newest thing. It's made from apricot pits.

"You know how these foreign countries are." She shakes her head. "It's bound to get here any day now."

"What if it doesn't? What will we do?" I want her to make other plans. Something else to count on.

"Well, they discover new things every day. Every day he has another chance. Someone is working on a cure right now."

"But what if we don't hear about it? What if it's too late?" I can't stand for it to be too late. I want my own plan, too.

"Honey, we have the best doctors I can find. The best." Mom doesn't think they're all in cahoots against her today. She turns in to the parking lot for the cleaners and shuts the engine off.

170

We're parked beneath some bare trees. The pavement buckles where their roots have grown up. A bird is hopping along the bark, down low.

Mom gets out of the car and starts yanking clothes from the back. She goes on talking. "He's going to be just fine, you'll see. I wouldn't be able to go on another day if I didn't think that. I wouldn't be able to cope. You've just got to believe in miracles. I do. I do believe in miracles." Her voice throws with the wind catching the tree branches, and it sounds extra bright, like it always does when she wants me to believe her.

Radioactive Gold

Mom no longer polishes her nails, and I miss seeing her do that. I miss the way she used to wash her underthings out for the government job, and hang them over the tub rail to dry. I liked going in the bathroom and secretly touching the long brown stockings with their darker bands at the toes and thighs, the shimmery slips and tiny, scratchy lace underwear. But Mom has quit the office to work the machines. She says she doesn't need any frills when she's working like a man all day. After school, whenever Jamie complains, I go along and help.

"Ellis found something," Mom whispers when she comes into my bed at night. "Something new. Something so special, he'll have to be kind of quarantined to get it. But the doctors are setting it up right now."

"What is it?" I roll over and my eyes hurt from the hall light. She doesn't say if I've been sleepwalking again. She smells of Jean Naté and beer.

"Now, I don't want you to go around saying it. If Grandma found out she'd have a fit. She'd get scared because it's radioactive. And you know how old-fashioned she is about that."

"Radioactive?" I feel old-fashioned, too. But then I feel a pinch of hope.

"Gold! Can you believe it? Radioactive gold," Mom says. "They're going to put him on the top floor of Mercy. Only doctors with lead shields can work on him there. You know, for protection. But it's okay. They're just going to give him this tiny bit. This little eensy bit at a time."

I cover my eyes with my arm and breathe. "Will it hurt?"

"You know Daddy. He wants to do it. He's going to go on trying everything until he's well. And this might be just the ticket. Radioactive *gold*," she repeats. "Doesn't that sound lucky? Doesn't that sound like the miracle we've been waiting for?"

I come home from school and the house is dim, the drapes shut. The furniture looks dusty in the shadows. Like nobody lives here at all. I sit on the couch and the plastic screeches and sighs. Mom has always liked this couch. When she got rid of the old green one, she said plastic was the newest thing. But I still miss the soft fabric when I lean back.

The air feels heavy and smells bad, like medicine. I jump when the roof creaks. Where is he? I don't hear him breathing. Or shifting in the bed. I get the shakes, listening to nothing. Listening so hard the silence moves out around me like a wall.

Then I remember. He's getting radioactive gold today.

When Ellis comes home full of radioactive gold, Boomer will not go in to see him. He stands outside the bedroom door and plants his feet. "Go on, Boomer," I say. "Please. You'll hurt his feelings if you don't."

Boomer is cute and funny and easy to hug. He always makes Ellis smile.

"No." He shakes his head. "I won't. And don't call me Boomer anymore."

"What's the matter? What are you scared of?"

"Nothing. I don't want to."

"Son?" Ellis calls. "Is that you?"

I shove my brother from behind and he turns and slugs me. He runs scared into his room and the door slams.

I go into Mom and Ellis's room and smooth the new silky quilt Mom bought for their bed. Smooth and smooth it. "Where's Boomer?" Ellis says. "Where's my boy?"

"He doesn't want us to call him Boomer anymore," I say. "I guess he's growing up."

"All of you are growing up," says Ellis, "too fast."

The Boat

You'd never guess that where the Sears store sits was once a field where a white horse used to run. I remember how Mom would see that horse in the field, and lick her thumb and stamp her palm for luck. Now in Sears we walk down the wide aisles touching things, lifting them as we go, to see the price tags, even though Mom says she doesn't really care about the price. We're Christmas shopping.

"We're going to have the best Christmas ever. We'll put it on the charge card," Mom says. "I'm going to get him one of these new Polaroid cameras," she says. "He's always interested in the latest things. I'm going to get him his boat—of course not the sailboat, we couldn't afford that; besides, where would we store it?" She giggles behind her hand. "But a little boat, a little skiff, that he can putter around in. Won't that be great?"

Mom's voice goes jittery; she doesn't look too steady on her feet. When she stumbles she says it's her high heels. She keeps walking through the aisles, looking up and down as if she's about to meet someone she knows, and grabbing things to buy. Over our heads the ceiling has green tinsel floating down in glittered loops. On the main aisle a plastic Santa waves with a glowy light inside his belly.

"Oh," Mom says and stops in front of the plastic trees. "This, too." She examines a white one, taller than she is. It's full of red and green balls. "But I won't do it like that. I'll do it all aqua instead. Aqua and white. It will be beautiful."

On Christmas morning we have the plastic tree with the aqua balls, the white-spangled limbs. We have dozens of presents heaped below the tree. Jamie and I get transistor radios, and there are bikes for Nick and Neal. "I thought we were broke," Jamie says, and Mom puts a finger to her lips.

"I bought out the store." She laughs when Ellis looks at her. "Try your camera." Ellis hasn't taken moving pictures of Christmas since he got too sick for Davey, Sarah, and April to come, but he tries his camera. It's hard to believe it will develop a picture right in front of us, even when we've seen the commercials a hundred times on TV.

He tells us to line up by the tree, and takes us from the couch, sitting down. He's still in his pajamas, but it doesn't seem unusual

174

today, on a holiday. He clicks the Polaroid's shutter and the film winds out like a tongue. He strips the tongue and pulls it apart and the film smell leaks out. We crowd around to watch ourselves forming by the tree. First like shadows moving and darkening, then with the lines coloring in. Our faces are the last to show.

On Christmas afternoon we load the new skiff on top of the station wagon and Mom drives us to the river. It's cold, but the sky is blue, and I think of that time we had Christmas in summer, with Sarah, Davey, and April, before things changed.

We step out of the car onto a spit of beach, and Ellis holds his face to the sun and smiles. He points out a blue heron to Nick, cupping his hands around Nick's ears and swiveling his head so he'll follow its flight. He keeps hold of Neal's hand. He can't help lift the skiff, but Jamie and Mom and I do it for him. We lower it in the water. Then we help him walk down the bank and climb aboard.

We sit Nick and Neal up front with orange life jackets. Mom in the center. Jamie and I push off. The skiff glides out when we jump in. Ellis cranks the motor and it splutters and starts. We chug out past the cold shadows thrown by the cottonwoods and shaggy eucalyptus. Mom grips the boat's sides. Her smile is thin. "Be careful! Watch out!" she says when anyone moves. I wish she'd wear a life jacket, too, but she never wears one, or seat belts, either. She says they're too confining, and that it's like expecting to be in an accident, preparing for one that way.

The motor makes *pauka pauka* sounds. It smells like gas. "We're okay," Ellis says. "This is a stable little thing." He rocks us from side to side until we dip back and forth.

"Be careful," Mom warns. Her knuckles turn white clutching the boat.

"You won't drown, Mom," Nick tells her. "I'll save you."

"Me too!" Neal agrees.

"Of course I won't drown. I'm not even thinking about that, silly." Mom's eyes rest on Ellis, waiting. She looks as if her heart will stop if he doesn't like the boat. Her heart will stop if he dies. Ellis winks and opens the throttle. The skiff tips up and skims faster. Mom grips the edge again.

"Slow down!" she begs. "Ellis!" But she's laughing now.

And I see what Mom knows. She was right about Christmas. In the little boat, Ellis keeps steering. I sit backwards so I can tell. The radioactive gold worked a tiny miracle. Ellis is happy. His eyes are narrowed, his shirt slaps across his skeleton chest. The river water splashes up brilliant behind him. And for now, nothing hurts.

Cool Air

The summer I turn twelve it gets hot early. Ellis sweats, lying in bed. Their room with the skin-diver wallpaper, the seashell lamp and curtains, reminds me of the ocean, but it's still too hot. Ellis tries to get up and fix our swamp cooler. He crabs up the ladder that Jamie and I hold. I'm scared, watching him on the roof. He plants his feet so slow, and he doesn't stay up there long.

"It's not getting water," he tells Jamie when he comes down. "I can't fix it right now. I don't feel well enough. You'll have to run the hose to it three times a day. Otherwise we'll just have hot wind coming in."

Jamie stands flat against the wall where the shade is. "Three times a day?" He stares at Ellis like he asked him to swallow poison.

"That's what I said." Ellis goes over to the faucet and slowly connects the hose. "Just climb up there and fill the pan." He hands the hose to Jamie.

"What about Cassie?"

"Cassie's going with Mom to fill the machines, remember?" Ellis retrieves his cane from the shade and moves to the back door. The Candys' cat is panting in our flower bed. Ellis stops and pats him, then goes in.

"He acts like I'm his slave," Jamie complains when the door closes. "Do this, do that. He doesn't care if I have other things going on. I have to work for Reece if I'm going to pay for lessons. Turn this on when I get up there."

I wait until he's halfway up and then I rattle the ladder.

"Hey!" he shouts, grabbing hold.

"Three times. Just don't forget."

"Ha." Jamie grips the roof edge and climbs on the house. He stands up and runs to the ridge as easily as if he's walking flat ground. He's wearing a peach-colored shirt, something no other boy will do. Up there it looks pink against the gray-blue sky. "There's no way I'm staying home for this!" he shouts.

Mexico

"I was saving it, but I'm going to tell him now. About the medicine in Mexico." Mom says the same thing over and over in my bedroom at night. "It's better than that gold stuff. In the end, that just made him worse."

"I thought they never answered."

"They will." Her voice sounds hard and metallic in the darkness of my room, like someone's beside her, threatening her with a gun. Tonight she smells like gardenias and the fuzzy smell of her nightgown. Her hair snaps with electricity when she moves. I can see the sparks traveling through the air, tiny bursts like sparklers.

"What about the Mayo Clinic?" I say. "Can't you try them again?"

"They don't know everything there. All those fancy doctors."

"But maybe they have something new by now."

"Hush," she says. "Don't worry about it. This Mexico thing is better."

"But they haven't even written, and it's a foreign country."

Mom frowns. "That's just it. Here, they won't let you try things, they want their money first, and things like this that are new, that work, it takes away from the doctors' pay."

"But why don't the doctors here want to cure him? If it's such a great thing, this medicine, why don't we have it, too?"

"You don't understand, honey. Someday you'll understand. It's complicated."

I'm quiet a while, thinking. I feel tight with the possibility of another cure. I want to know how long it will take until he's up again, until he's not so skinny. I see myself giving him the pills—would it be pills?—and him smiling when he swallows them, feeling a little better every time. She's right, I don't understand.

"I pray," I say. "Every night."

"That's good, sweetheart. I don't know what I'd do without

you." She grabs my hand in the dark. I don't tell Mom the private part, that when I pray I imagine myself as God might see me, kneeling on my floor. I always push the rug away so it hurts. And even though praying sometimes feels as foolish as believing in a gypsy curse, I think of sad things, like the Unicef children with their swollen bellies and begging eyes, that will make me cry when I ask it. Because if there is a God, he might listen better if he sees I'm serious. I decide to work the trip to Mexico into my prayers.

I picture a trip to Mexico, which seems farther away than last time. Ellis will have to sleep in the back of the station wagon, with the seat down; there won't be room for Jamie, Nick, or Neal. We can't leave them home alone because Jamie might not watch them right. We'll have to get Grandma to come and stay. The driving part will be easy. I can already feel the air in through the windows, I can feel how the cups of sound will blot out everything else. We'll stop to eat at drive-ins and bring Ellis's food right to the car. We'll buy him lots of milk shakes.

Mom drives me out to a long, low building by the river. There was a thundershower, and the clouds are breaking up. The sun strikes silver across the water, which roils like it's full of restless fish, just below the surface.

"Look at that." She pulls onto the shoulder and turns the car off. She points to the building. She takes a big gulp of beer. She's drinking it fast, and she hardly worries about the cops anymore. "That's where the doctors want me to put him." Her voice moves up and away like a kite that no one's holding. "So I wouldn't have to watch it, is what they said. But I'll be damned if I'm going to let anybody take him away. I'll be damned!"

She doesn't look at me. She talks out the window, staring at the low building, and hating it. The sign out front says Miller's Convalescent Home.

We both start to cry, and I want to tell her I love her for being crazy, for not believing any of it. I'm glad she'd never put him here. She starts the car and guns the engine and says over the roar, "We'll move our big bed into your room. And your little bed into ours. That way a hospital bed will fit. We'll get a wheelchair and a bedpan. And he's going to have to take shots."

Chess

Mom has to give Ellis his shots, so the doctor teaches her how. He comes to Diamond Street and into Ellis and Mom's room and shuts the three of them in there. When Mom comes out her face is gray. "I can do it," she says. "I can." But she looks scared because a shot done wrong can kill him.

Ellis needs his shots every few hours, whenever he starts to hurt. Mom does the vending-machine route and rushes home in between stops, always at the last minute as if she can't really believe she'll have to be the one. She hurries in breathless. Her eyes are pale because she's given up wearing makeup. Her hair is pulled back off her forehead and sticking out every which way from under the elastic headband.

She stops at the bedroom door right before she goes in. And rearranges her face into her best, frozen smile.

Moss from the diving club comes to visit, but he's the only one. Mom says he understands because he's sick too, with diabetes.

He always talks to Mom first, privately, watching her with his watery blue eyes and squeezing her hands in his hands. "If you need any help. Anything at all," he tells her. Then he goes in to see Ellis.

Moss and Ellis play chess by laying the board on the bed. Moss sits in a chair and Ellis stays in bed. They shut the bedroom door. It's quiet in there. Sometimes their voices come out in low rumbles and sometimes there's only the sound of the chessmen being moved from place to place.

Haircut

Mom stays in the bathroom a long time. When she comes out her hair's cut short-short, like a boy's. She's got jagged bangs and her neck is showing. She runs her fingers through what's left of her hair. She looks strange, younger. Jamie and I don't say anything.

Neal runs down the hall, and when he sees her he stops and stares. "Why'd you cut your hair like that? I hate it."

"Neal!" I grab him by the neck. "Take that back." He looks confused.

Mom goes over to the mirror above the couch. "Maybe I got it too short," she says, like she just noticed.

I shake Neal and he twists away and runs back into his room, shouting to Nick about Mom's hair. Nick runs out to see, but he never says what he thinks about anything.

Mom drops to the couch and cries. "I did get it too short."

I sink down next to her. "Don't cry, Mom." Her hands are trembly. The way she looks at me, I could be from another planet.

"Move over," Jamie says. He takes my place and wraps his arms around her. "They're plebeians," he says. "They don't appreciate new things."

"Oh, God—" Mom hides her face between her hands.

"Peasants and plebeians," Jamie says and he presses his forehead against Mom's skinned neck.

Solitaire

Aunt Larue shows up on Diamond Street. Mom says she's come to help us. She brings a man named Ted who she calls her husband when everyone knows that's a lie. Ted drives a truck and pulls a silver trailer, but the two of them sleep in the guest bedroom instead.

Aunt Larue hasn't changed a bit. She's still the same old sourpuss. She still drinks beer for breakfast. Little tiny Coors beers that each come in a can with the new pop-top. When you pull the pop-top off it makes a metal ring that fits around your finger.

When I see Larue drinking her breakfast beer my heart yanks. At first she does the laundry and cooks our dinner and I don't have to do it, but then one day Ted disappears, and after that, Larue won't help anymore. Instead she plays solitaire at the dining room table, smoking Salems and piling tiny Coors cans in the trash.

One day Aunt Larue switches from tiny to tall Coors. She's sitting on our front porch when I get home from the store on my bike. Her face is squinched up with sun and a long skirt wraps her knees. A white ruffled blouse slides off her bony shoulders.

182

Larue has sharp eyes in her wrinkled face. Thick white fingernails and bumpy yellow skin. Her skinny legs have dark purple blots like spilled ink, with veins running in and out of them.

She doesn't look happy to see me.

"Your swamp cooler's busted again," she says.

"Is Mom home?"

"She's doing the shot. Why hasn't anybody fixed it?"

"Jamie is supposed to keep it filled with water."

"Well, he's not here."

I can tell she wants me to do it, but I'm not as good at walking the roof as Jamie.

"Ellis is suffering in this heat," she says. "Belle should get a new cooler."

I tell her we can't afford one.

"Hunh." Aunt Larue snorts. She narrows her eyes at me. She burps.

Mom opens the door. "He's asleep," she says about Ellis. She comes outside and stands next to Larue. "Are the boys home yet?"

"Sit," says Larue. "Nick and Neal are playing across the street."

Mom sits on the porch step. "I'm so glad you're here," she says in a little-kid voice to Larue.

"I know." Aunt Larue looks sympathetic. "You got to fix the cooler, though. It's only going to get hotter."

Mom pulls her shirt away from her sweating skin. "I would, but I overloaded the Sears card at Christmas."

Larue nods. She reaches into the porch shade and brings a beer from her six-pack. "Try this," she says. "You're losing weight."

"I can't eat." Mom takes the beer. She cracks the can and drinks.

"I'll make you something," I say. "I'll fix iced tea."

"No," says Mom, "I'll just sit here." She drinks the beer down, even though usually she says tall Coors are too much for her. When she finishes it Aunt Larue hands her another one.

Larue has forgotten to make lunch for Nick and Neal's day camp. I hurry and throw things into their pails, turn off the TV where they're sitting slurping the last of their Lucky Charms.

"Brush your teeth!" I shout. It drives me crazy when they won't.

Nick wipes his mouth with the back of his hand. He pushes Neal out the door. I chase them onto the lawn and their lunch pails bang when they run. Their T-shirts move white into the bright, bright day, away from me.

"I can cook," I tell Mom. "I can watch Nick and Neal. She isn't doing anything but drinking beer." Mom and I are alone in the kitchen. Larue is across the street at Janet Candy's.

"Just give her a chance," Mom says. "She's doing all right. And Ellis likes the things she cooks."

"*When* she cooks," I say. I shake my head. Mom doesn't seem to notice that all Larue does is play solitaire with the radio turned to country music. She flips the cards from her hand onto the snaking rows and frets about the swamp cooler. And when the radio plays "Counting Flowers on the Wall," she cranks up the volume and cries.

184

The Talk

I feel like Neal, afraid to go into Ellis's room. But Ellis tells me to sit on the edge of the bed, which is a good sign. When he's feeling bad I can't do this or he flinches from the pain. Only right after his shot he feels okay, he feels better. Mom says we're lucky the drugs don't affect his mind. He sits up a little for me to fix his pillows.

"You look better today," I say.

"No. I don't." He holds out his hand. "Look at this." I look at the bones and skin. The skin is greenish, not like normal. "I'm not going to make it, Snikelfritz," he says.

I pretend I don't know what he means. I look down at my bare feet. I painted my toenails a couple of weeks ago, but the paint is chipped and peeling.

"I can't eat anymore," he says.

"Can't you try?" I look at him.

"What I mean is, food doesn't do me any good. It just goes right through me. They can't cure somebody who doesn't have a stomach."

"But they know all kinds of new things now. They—"

"That's your mother talking. There aren't going to be any miracle cures."

I look back at my feet. I don't want to cry in front of him. Then he'll know he's right. If I give up, too. I make myself think about my nail polish. Of changing the color from pink to red, like Mom used to wear.

"It's going to reach my brain next," he says.

Red. Red. Red.

"And that will be it."

This little piggy went to market. This little piggy stayed

home. This—

"I wish they'd put me to sleep. I hate doing this to you guys."

"That's crazy! That's what they do to dogs!" My toes blur.

"Okay, come on. Don't cry. You're a big girl. I can be honest with you."

But you promised you'd get better! And I've tried so hard!

Ellis's hand moves slowly down his slicked-back hair. "Do you remember the day you thought it was going to be the end of the world? Remember how you got busy and forgot to be scared?"

"And we went down the elevator underground." I wipe my eyes. I chance a look at him. *And you put me on the dolly and I fell back, but you caught me at the last minute like you always do.*

"That's right." He smiles.

But who will catch me if you're gone?

"We've had some good adventures, haven't we?"

He's watching the ceiling. Like he's talking to me and he isn't.

"You're a big help to your mother," he says. "And you're doing a fine job with the boys."

"It's no big deal. I can take care of them."

"They'll be all right," he says to the ceiling. "They're young. And Jamie. He has his dancing. But your mother—" He sighs and presses his head into the pillow, where he hardly makes a dent. "It won't be easy for her."

"What should I do?" I don't know what to do.

His face tightens. "Just keep an eye on her."

"All right."

"You know why I eat when it doesn't do me any good?" Ellis lifts his knees under the sheet and his hands settle onto them.

I shake my head.

"Because I like the taste. Can you believe it? I still like the taste."

"I have to go to the bathroom," Ellis says. "You have to get the bedpan." His voice is sorry and I swallow hard. I pull the pan from its place in the bathtub and carry it into the room. He tries to lift himself, but he's so weak he can't. He can't lift himself and slide the pan under too, so I do that for him. But I turn my head at the last minute. I walk out of the room.

I wait until he says, "I'm ready," before I go back in. His face is flushed. "I smell," he says.

I help him wipe. I help him lie down. I don't gag until I'm safe in the bathroom, dumping the pan.

Shots Done Wrong

Mom still isn't home when it's time for Ellis's shot. "Where is she?" Ellis wails, groping for the bedside clock. "Is she with Larue? Is she drinking?"

"No," I lie, because I don't really know if she's drinking or not. But if she's with Larue they probably are. "She's checking on things. She'll be back." I call the stations where we have our machines, but I can't find her. And besides, she didn't take the station wagon.

Ellis's hands jerk, gripping the sheet. "Cass—you'll have to do it for me! I can't take it any longer!" He's shouting this; his eyes jump around. His stuttery hands. I hear a car and run to the window, but it isn't Mom. Nick, Neal, and Carmen Candy are kicking a ball in the front yard, moving forward like three people sewn together. I turn back. Ellis is sweating bad. His skin looks like old chicken skin. His eyes beg me. I've done the bedpan and cleaned up after he's sick and lots of other things, but I don't want to do this.

I pick up the plastic syringe and uncover the needle. There are a bunch of other syringes in the drawer by the bed. We're supposed to throw them away, but sometimes the boys like to play with them.

Outside my brothers call to each other. Their voices sound far off. I take his arm. There are dozens of needle welts in his skin. I follow these carefully, like another explorer's map. "Here," he says, and I jab hard. The medicine disappears from the syringe. *A shot done wrong can kill him.* The doctor's words crack me like thunder.

But he's dying anyway.

Ellis stares at the ceiling again, waiting. His pupils go big and small, like the peephole in Nick's telescope. Like he's trying to see out beyond the roof, way up into the sky, where God is. He closes his eyes. I make myself pop the needle out of the syringe and throw it away. Then I go into the bathroom and throw up.

The Fight

Mom doesn't come back for dinner. She doesn't come back in time for Ellis's next shot, which I have to give him again. I feed

Nick and Neal and put them to bed. A motor rumbles outside and I run to the window, but it's just Reece, bringing Jamie home in his little red sports car. Jamie comes in and Ellis hears him. He calls out to him to load the station wagon for tomorrow's route. Ellis is still worried about keeping the machines filled right. Jamie says okay, he will, and goes in his room and shuts the door.

I stay in my room, reading *Lorna Doone*. I always get the biggest book I can find, to make it last. I hear a scraping noise outside and open my curtain and there's Ellis, dressed, loading the station wagon himself. I think I must be dreaming. He never gets up anymore.

I jump off the bed and *Lorna Doone* crashes to the floor. Outside he's pushing things into the back of the wagon from the dolly. I don't know how he got it loaded. I don't know how he got it down the driveway. For a minute I think, if he's up, maybe he will get cured. But he can hardly lift the boxes.

"Daddy, what are you doing?"

He doesn't answer right away. His mouth twists. "I just lay in that bed and worry."

It's pitch dark. None of the neighbors have their porch lights on; I can only see him in the little car light, his chin and part of his cheek. But I worry that someone will notice how bad he looks. Then I'm mad at myself for thinking this. A sprinkler is going *chit chit chit*. There's a breeze from the river. The leaves make their gathering sound.

I try to take a box, but he jerks it away. His breath comes out too short. I'm afraid he'll fall in the street and I won't be able to get him back to bed.

"I'll get Jamie," I say. "Wait."

He keeps on loading.

"Wait for Mom, then. She'll be home any minute."

"Don't kid yourself. I know where she is." He lurches, holding a box, and drops it down on the tailgate.

"I'm going to call her right now," I say, which is another lie. I don't know where to call.

"I'm sick." Ellis hits the box with his hand. "I can't help that. I can't help it!"

I look at the box, as if it knows all the answers and will tell us what to do. I remember the way he used to come home from work and kiss her, sweeping her back, making her blush. I want to kill her.

"She's scared," I say, and I know it's true. Because I'm scared, too. I'm scared that Ellis talks to me like I'm her, that *I feel* like I'm her—as if Mom and I have traded places.

Ellis pushes at the box, but he's too weak to make it move.

"She'll just drink," he says, "after."

"How am I supposed to know where they are?" Jamie glares at me. "She's a grown-up." He's in the guest bedroom, at the desk, trying to draw pictures of Jayne Mansfield, the newest movie star he's in love with.

"If you'd done what he asked, this wouldn't have happened," I say.

"I always do what he asks. I'm sick of doing what he asks."

"No, you don't. You're always trying to get out of things."

"Why shouldn't I?" He starts shading in Jayne Mansfield's hair. "Those machines are a waste of time. He's leaving us with a mess."

"Don't say that."

"What, that he's dying? You're as bad as *she* is."

I grab the paper and it rips under the pencil lead. Jamie leaps up and takes a swing at me, and I fly at him and push him onto the bed. He falls with a surprised *oomph* and the headboard bangs the wall. His eyes bulge.

Then I'm on top of him, hitting him fast, over and over, and his face balls up like it's going to explode.

"You're crazy!" Jamie hollers. "Get off me!"

I *am* crazy. Even when he tries to cover his face with his arms and then hits me back, I don't feel him. I only feel me, the part of me I hide away, moving fast but moving in slow motion, too. A light behind my eyes blurs and flashes.

"He's not dying! He's not!" I shout. "You just want him to! You just hope he will!"

I stop. Ellis is calling. "Cassie? Jamie? What's going on?"

"Now look!" I try to slide off Jamie, but he grabs my ankle.

"You little witch!" he says. He scrambles up and wraps me from behind, spins me around, and pushes me into the hall. We're fighting and then we both go still because Ellis is standing there.

"What's the matter with you two?" He lifts his cane off the floor. For the second time tonight, I'm surprised to see him up.

"It's her fault. She started it. Look." Jamie shows him two red welts on his cheek.

Ellis's cane comes down with a little thud. But he's way too weak to punish us. He looks at me, disappointed. "Go to your room, Cass."

I can't believe this. "But he—"

"Don't argue. Get."

I wish he had the strength to hit me with his cane, to make

191

me go. Then, I'd do anything he said. I run into the living room. No lights are on. I crouch in the corner behind his easy chair. Ellis is talking to Jamie. Outside the curtain are the silhouettes of trees and rooftops, and beyond them, pale stars. But where I am it's like a dark throat, squeezing.

"Cassie." I hear shuffling and Ellis is standing by the chair.

I dig my forehead into my knees. "He should have loaded the car for you," I say.

"Come out here," Ellis says.

"He should have."

"I know. I'm sorry. Comeer now."

"I hate him!"

"No, you don't."

I uncurl, get up, and go over slow. He looks down at me. He holds out his arms and I fall into them, wrap my hands around his back, and he feels like my dad, only thinner. So thin. His bones are right beneath his shirt, cradling his heart's short beats, and I feel cheated by his getting up. Like he's a ghost already, just held together by his clothes.

Ellis doesn't stand there long. He gets too shaky and I have to help him back to bed. Then I wait up for Mom. You'd think she'd know. Why doesn't she know when to come home? I sit on the couch watching light creep around the edges of the curtain when a car goes by in the street.

Finally I get up and tiptoe into Mom and Ellis's room. I stand next to the hospital bed. In the dark his wheelchair gleams from the corner. Ellis's eyes look open, right into me. But when I kneel down and put my head on his chest he grunts, surprised, like he was asleep after all.

"Belle?"

"No, it's me."

"Is she home?"

"Not yet, Daddy."

"Look what I'm leaving my family with," he wails. "Belle will have to raise our boys. And what about Sarah, April, and Davey? What about Jamie?" His eyes find me. "And you? You're just a little girl."

"You told me I was grown up!"

His hand snakes up and tries to steal my nose. I wish I had the right words. Magic words to erase what he's been thinking. The breath goes out of me. I am a little girl.

All I say is, "I love you, Daddy! I don't want you to die!"

His hand cups the back of my head, steadier now. "I love you, too. Remember that. I'll always be your dad." But his voice is hoarse and cracked, like a man who's never talked before.

Butcher Knife

Mom comes into my room early. The first thing I think is, she's home. She sits on the end of my bed. Her hair isn't combed. She looks younger this morning, except that under her eyes the skin is dark. She touches her face, her hair; she twists her wedding ring. She sits up straight as if for a picture.

"He asked me to send for Grandma again," she says. "He said, 'You'd better get Mom today. It's time.'" She looks at me, incredulous. "I called Janet. She said she'll go. Jamie will have to go too, to show her the way."

She doesn't say anything about yesterday. Yesterday was a million years ago. I don't say anything either. I just move toward her, sink slow against her. I rest my head on her chest. Her heart is twitching under her nightgown. We sit together for a minute, then she jumps up and paces around my little room, and her hands do their dance again, in her hair and at her throat.

The siren wails loud down the block. Two men in white knock on the door and Mom lets them in. I watch from the hall while they move Ellis. How they lift him easily onto the stretcher and strap him down. Jamie comes out, but I just look past him.

Outside, the neighbors stand in a half circle, close to the back of the ambulance, as if they're about to crawl in. Not just the ones we know, Winston and Matt, the Catholics and Louis, but people from all up and down Diamond Street, people who've never seemed to notice our house before. They stare at Ellis, and the blinking light rubs across their skin.

I push through them. Mom is bent over, talking to Ellis. When they lift him inside and shut the doors, she does a strange thing. She stands up and looks at the neighbors and smiles as if she thinks someone's taking her picture again.

There are so many adults at the hospital. Jamie's dancing teacher, Reece, and Moss from the diving club. They all stare at me when I walk in.

"Cassie?" says Reece, and "Where do you think you're going?" Moss asks.

They don't want me in Ellis's room. But I just keep walking.

Mom and I sit by Ellis all day. I hold his hand, and once he squeezes back, turns his head and looks at me. Instead of blinking, his eyes just stay open, as if they never mean to close.

—

Moss drives me home from the hospital. I don't talk. He's got the radio on and the music punches. Buildings rush up. Car lights. The lights cover my skin and press my eyes, jabbing and poking and breathing.

No lights are on at our house. "You okay?" says Moss.

"I'm okay." I climb out of his car, and our grass is tall at my ankles. Jamie and I have been taking turns mowing, but Jamie forgot. I shut the car door and after a while Moss drives away. When he's gone I look up at the stars. Usually you can't see so many. Around each one wavers a little halo of mist.

The house is dark inside, too, but I hear Larue at the table. The dry snap of cards. She sets one down and then another. She belches and hums a cowboy song.

"Ouch," she says when I flip on the light.

"You're playing in the dark."

"I go by feel." She snaps another card.

"Where are Nick and Neal?"

She shrugs. "What's-her-name. Down the street." She lifts her Coors.

I don't know who she means. I have to call the neighbors up and down the block until I find them at Mrs. Carlson's.

"They're asleep," Mrs. Carlson whispers. "Should I wake them?"

"I guess not," I whisper back as if I might wake them up from here. It feels like I've been gone for days. There's a mess in the kitchen, dirty pans and plates and chili spilled on the stovetop, scalded and congealed. Sauce everywhere, splattered like blood.

"How's your mom, she okay?" Mrs. Carlson says.

195

"She's coming home. Later." I can't say *after*. I can't.

"Oh. Well. You come over here if you need to." I imagine Mrs. Carlson's. Her clean kitchen. Her two little kids tucked in bed. She'd make up the sofa for me, with fresh sheets smelling sweet from the line.

I look at the kitchen mess and my bones clack. My insides burn up coming home to this. Having to call Mrs. Carlson.

I hang up and start on the kitchen, scrubbing the baked-on chili. The smell makes my stomach flip.

"They should be at home tonight," I say. Tonight of all nights. I scrub harder.

Aunt Larue mumbles, hunched over her cards. "Who?" she says.

"Nick and Neal!" Scrubbing until my knuckles ache.

"Such a little mother."

The dishrag flies out of my hand before I can stop it. It hits the side of her cheek and her face slides sideways at me.

"Why, you—!"

I surprise myself by laughing. I'm that crazy girl again and I can't stop being her. I'm the girl who hid the wishing-well card and killed her own goldfish and fought with Jamie and tries to be Mom and is mad, mad.

Larue stumbles up. She kicks the chair away. "I'll kill you," she says. She grabs my hair and pulls. I smell the dank space under her arms.

I stop laughing. I twist away and lose a fistful of hair.

I feel for the kitchen drawer and search until my hands find something solid. I hold it up for her to see.

Larue's mouth falls open.

"You little monster!" Her breath comes ragged.

"That's right!" I roar. "I'm a monster!"

The phone rings. Larue tries to answer it, but I charge at her. "Get away! Now!" Flames are shooting through me. I'm so crackling hot I catch the room on fire.

"Jesus!" Larue backs up. She looks terrified. "Your mother will hear about this!"

"Go in your room and don't come out!" When I step toward her my aunt turns and runs.

I pick up the phone when the door slams shut. Now that the ringing has stopped, I'm caught in the silence. I know it's Mom.

"Cassie?" she says. "Oh, God!" She doesn't have to say any more. She doesn't have to tell me. I look at my hand. I'm surprised to find I'm holding Ellis's butcher knife. I lay it carefully down.

Limo Ride

Mom goes all out on the funeral by spending the money from Ellis's life insurance policy. She buys a silver coffin with a satin lining. She buys big sprays of flowers. She rents the funeral parlor with pretty stained-glass windows and thick red carpet on West Street. Jamie asks for a limousine to take us to the gravesite, so she rents that, too. For a few days, we feel rich.

Ellis lies in the silver coffin surrounded by cold-smelling flowers. The stained-glass windows tint the air blue, and the blue feels thick with silence and whispers. We sit on oak benches, hidden from the other mourners by black mesh curtains, like we're somebody important. I'm wearing a pair of Mom's gloves. Little sewn ridges run along the tops of each finger and end just beyond my knuckles. I trace these ridges while the minister speaks.

April, Davey, and Sarah are sitting somewhere else, with their mother. Mom did not want to see her, so it's just us behind the curtains. Mom is between Nick and Neal. Then come Grandma and Jamie, and I'm on the other side. We're like a small island of people, with me on the edge.

We take the limousine to the graveyard. I stare out the window as the streets reel by. The hearse drives ahead of us. Jamie has the little seat behind the driver, sitting backward, and holding Grandma's hand. Her old face is saggy with tears. Neal clutches Mom, and Nick grips my hand.

The limo rides smooth. I imagine it from the outside, black and fussy-looking. And I can see out, but I'm so far back in the seat that no one can see me.

When they lower the coffin down in the hole and push the dirt on top, I can't get my breath, and the sound of it stays in my ears. Everyone cries except Nick, and I worry about that. He's only seven; he should cry. Neal slips his hand out of Mom's when we turn to leave. "I'm sleeping here," he says, "in case Daddy wakes up and wants some dinner." Jamie is the one who finally picks him up and carries him away.

Then we're home and the day's so long. People act like it's a party, coming over and bringing food. Moss from the diving club sits by Mom and stares at her with his watery blue eyes. Jamie stares at Moss. All of a sudden Jamie's trying to do everything right to be the man of the family. He looks shrunken in his Sunday suit. His face is thin. He helps Grandma fill her plate and talks to all the grown-ups. I smell the heaping plates and want to throw up. It gets hot in the house and Jamie goes to fix the cooler, like he can make up for things. I come near Mom and she grabs my hand and holds it. I think I should cry too, but I don't. I don't even get mad again. I'm blank inside, nothing, except for the sharpness of everyone else's feelings.

We've kept the drapes shut, and cold air is pouring in from the cooler now. Nick and Neal run outside and I'm standing at the door before I hear myself yelling, "Get back in here! Both of you!"

"Never mind, Cass," says Janet Candy. "They're too young to understand."

Nick and Neal stop running and point up at the roof, and I step outside and look. Jamie's sitting on the ridge, sobbing, holding the hose in both hands as if he'll never let it go.

I climb up the ladder and walk out shaky along the sloping roof. I sit down beside him. His pant legs are wet, and his good shoes.

"Jamie?"

He turns to me and his face is the loneliest face on earth. It's like looking into a mirror. "I didn't mean it," he says. "All those times I said I hated him. I didn't really hate him. I didn't really want him to die!"

"I know," I say. And I take the hose and throw it off the roof, and a stream of water slices across the sky.

Grief

Trying to sleep with this emptiness after Ellis dies is like being lost. It's like getting into bed a long time ago, with Geraldine from the 21 Club. Afraid the bed will close up, knowing I am Old Daddy's friend Angel, all twisted up and buried in concrete.

Part 4

"Now you're up shit creek without a paddle."
—*Janet Candy*

Sleeping Alone

The hospital bed is gone. Mom has her double bed back, but she won't sleep alone. At night she calls from her room, "Who wants to sleep with me? Who wants to keep me company?"

Sometimes just Neal and Nick do, and sometimes I come in. Mom won't let Jamie because he's too old. I take the side of the bed by the window, where Ellis used to sleep, watching the divers on the wallpaper sending their bubbles up and up to the surface. Watching them reach for their conch shells.

Mom's feet under the covers are like ice and they search out my feet. Our toes touch and her foot slides up the top of mine. She smells like all her smells, her gauzy nightgown, Jean Naté, and Aqua Net hairspray. When she thinks I'm asleep, she cries.

Now Jamie and I cook and clean together and watch out for Nick and Neal. It seems as if the house belongs to us, a moon that Mom revolves around, a little source of gravity that keeps her from floating off into space, being swallowed by some black hole.

She wants to sell the vending machines. She says she's tired of worrying about being busted into and how hard it is to keep any of the good locations, because somebody bigger always forces you out. "And the license fees," she wails, "how could Ellis not know about the license fees? We can't even pay the fine!"

"But we need the money from the machines," I say. "How else can we pay our bills?"

"I'll look for another job," she says. "With the government again. Where I can dress up for a change."

Mom signs up for a shorthand class. On Tuesday, Ellis's diving club friend, Moss, arranges for his wife, Martha, to go with her. Martha says she wants to get a job, too, now that her kids are older. She comes by for Mom at seven and Mom's still fidgeting with her clothes. Martha follows her around the house making helpful comments. "Your hair looks fine. You look fine. I don't think you'll need that jacket."

Mom stops in the hall on the way out the door. She pulls at her dress as if her skin feels tight. She waves to Aunt Larue, sorting her solitaire deck. Martha's still talking, heading across the porch. Mom rolls her eyes for me and we laugh. Mom always says in private that Martha has a face as long as George Washington's. But then I'm nervous, watching her out the picture window, the reluctant way she steps into Martha's car.

"I don't see how she stands it. Oh, my God, it was awful." Mom stumbles in the dark room and flips on the light. I sit up in her bed, blinking.

"What was awful?"

"I can't do it. I just can't do it. Writing a million little lines on paper. Maybe it's okay for someone like Martha. I just sat staring at them thinking, what has this got to do with me?" She stops and looks me over. "Are you losing weight?"

"No, and it's got to do with a job, remember? So we can make our house payment."

"Well, you look taller." She sits on the edge of the bed for me to unzip her. Then she stands and wriggles out of her dress. "And you *are* losing weight. You're not eating right. You've got to eat."

"You don't eat."

"That's different." She folds her dress across a chair back where she always piles her clothes. Even though it's been years since Jamie and I sneaked in here to dress up in her things, she still sometimes warns us that she knows where everything is, and how she first laid it there, so if we touch anything, she can tell. "You're not me," she says. I look away. I already know she's right, because Mom is sad on the outside, where everyone can see it, and I'm sad way underneath.

"Oh, God," she moans and sits back down in her slip. She pulls off her nylons, one at a time. Her slip and bra straps look tight, leave permanent grooves in her shoulders. "I really don't know how I'm going to stand that class."

"It'll be okay," I say. "You have to try it for a while. I mean, school is always hard." I don't know how to convince her.

"You don't understand." She starts her hands going. To her hair, her waist, her throat. "You just don't understand. That classroom. Sitting there for hours. And when I applied for the job, the office they showed me? All those little partition things? And hardly any windows. I just don't think I can do it!"

"What do you want to do?" My voice doesn't sound like me. It sounds like a parrot, shrieking.

"I don't know. I don't know!"

I lower my voice. "I'll rub your back if you lay down."

Mom stands up. She pads into the bathroom, comes back, and shuts the light off. She crawls into bed and stretches out, sighs. Her feet find my feet under the covers. I start making circles on her back.

"Don't say anything to Jamie yet. And especially not to Larue," she says. "Oh, Cass, what am I going to do?"

"It's only six weeks. Can't you do it for that long?" I plead.

She rolls over and looks at the ceiling. "Ten minutes is too much," she says.

Mom comes home late from shorthand class. I sit up in her bed, reading, until I hear the car in the drive. Then I shut off the light and scrunch under the covers. I listen to her fumbling her key in the lock and opening the front door. The phone rings. She picks it up. I know she's talking to Moss because of the way her voice swings up and down, like a chant. When she hangs up, she goes into the bathroom for a long time. I wait, watching the clock hands move from twelve to twelve-fifteen. My stomach's growling. Finally she comes in and flips on the light.

"How are the boys?" She kicks off her shoes and shows me her back. I grope at her zipper.

"I made dinner and put them to bed. Larue wouldn't help at all. Where've you been, anyway? It's after midnight."

"We went out after. For a drink. Did you eat?"

A hammer starts up in my chest. "No, and Martha doesn't drink."

"Not Martha." I can smell it on her now, and she moves clumsy. "Janet. I met Janet."

"Then you didn't go to class." The hammer thumps.

"Why aren't you eating, Cass?"

"Why aren't you going to class?"

"Don't you start. I've already gotten the third degree from *him*." She shimmies out of her dress and drops onto the bed. "He just wants Martha to go with me so he can spy on me. Ha. I know what he's after."

"He was Daddy's friend," I say. "People worry. Something

could have happened to you." *Thump. Thump. Thump.*

"I wouldn't defend him if I were you." Mom shuts her eyes. "He's a typical male." Out in the kitchen, the phone starts to ring again.

"Aren't you going to get it?" I say.

Mom sighs. "I'm not ready for that. Can't he see?" She lays there until the ringing stops.

"You forgot the light," I say.

"Get it, will you, honey?"

"Shit."

"Don't talk that way. Where did you learn to talk like that?"

"From you and Janet Candy!"

"Don't be silly. Where are you going?"

"I'm going in my own bed."

She sits up. "Don't go. Stay with me."

"I don't want to. I'm tired. I have to get up in the morning."

"You'll get up. I'll get you up. Please, honey."

I stare at her. The hammer keeps thumping. I'm trying to watch out for her, like I promised, but it's harder than I thought. It's like being five again, watching Old Daddy drink himself away from us. I'm twelve years old, but I feel like I'm a hundred.

She looks little, hunched up in her bed with the covers over her knees. Ellis was right. She's falling apart.

"Come on, now, shut off the light," she says. And the way she says this, I can tell she thinks I'm going to give in, because I always do. I shuffle over to the bed. I turn off the light and flop down. But I glare at the ceiling, reeling away from me in black splotches.

SMUD

Jamie argues with the SMUD man who wants to shut our gas off. The SMUD man is down in the little concrete well by the side of the house. He's got a lock on the meter. He's jotting numbers down on a pad.

"We don't have a father," Jamie says. "He died. And my mother's working day and night. It's not like she isn't working."

The SMUD man wears a green shirt and pants. A green billed cap. He squares his cap down on his head and keeps on writing. Sun across his slumped shoulders makes them glow.

"It's not like she can't pay any day," Jamie goes on. "Any day. If you'd just give us a break."

"I gave you a break last week, son." The SMUD man finishes writing and stands up. He cranks his arm behind him and pushes on his back. "Getting old," he says.

"But there's another fee to turn it back on," says Jamie. "That will make it harder to pay!"

"Hey, I only work for them. You want me to get fired?"

"You want us to freeze? Go hungry? How are we supposed to cook?" Jamie can be stubborn as a mule when he wants to.

"Pay your bill." The SMUD man climbs out of the little well and heads for his truck, but Jamie steps in front of him.

"One more week," he begs. "Please."

The man looks at Jamie and then at me. He looks at Nick and Neal, standing down by the street, watching. But Jamie's won.

"Jesus," the SMUD man says, and sighs.

The Letter

"Look at this notice," I say. "We're behind two months. We could lose the house."

"Oh, God." Mom takes a long drink of Aunt Larue's beer.

"I knew it!" says Larue and slaps the table, just like she's been waiting.

"So we have to pay it!" I'm afraid to look at Mom. Her crumpled face. I know she's afraid, too.

Aunt Larue's mouth pinches behind her fist and she belches loud. "There goes River City," she says.

Farm Labor

"I don't want you doing this," Mom says.

"Well, I'm going to," I tell her. "I can make ten dollars a day."

"There's nowhere to park." Mom is driving around and around the county building where you get your work permit. She eyes the shabby building that sits by the railroad tracks. "I'm just going to forget it," she says.

"Here. Go here." I point and she screeches the tires and slings the car into the loading zone.

She rakes at her hair. "I can't go in if we park here. I might have to move the car."

"I know."

"I don't want you going in alone." She studies the slouchy teenagers and the Mexican men on the sidewalk. "This is ridiculous. I need you at home. To watch the boys and cook."

"Larue is supposed to be doing that, remember?"

Mom turns her head to look at traffic and I jump out. I already have the permission slip she signed, so I go inside and get in line. The white girl ahead of me turns around, pops her gum, and stares.

"You picking tomatoes?" she asks. "How old are you?"

"Fifteen," I say. You have to be fifteen to get a work permit.

"Sure," she says, and grins.

After a long wait I'm at the counter. I'm worried the man behind the wavy glass will ask me how old I am, too. But he doesn't even look up. He just stamps my permit and tells me not to be late for the bus.

"If you're late, you're left," he says.

Nora, the white girl who was in line for a work permit, sits next to me on the farm-labor bus. Nora is on a diet. "I don't eat nothing but carrots, celery, and cucumber sandwiches," she says and stuffs her lunch bag under the seat. She confronts her reflection in the dusty window and tries to brush her hair. "If you're smart, you won't talk to any of these people," she adds. She thinks that the farm-labor workers are dirty. "And if you ever meet him, you'd better watch out for my brother, too," she says.

We're riding to the fields in a rumbly yellow school bus. Our seats are ripped and black smoke spits out the back. The sky out the broken window is gloomy yellow-gray.

"My brother has read the *Encyclopaedia Britannica* front to back," Nora says. "Doesn't matter. He's still a moron."

"My brother is a dancer," I say. "He's got talent."

"Is he cute?"

"He's got blue eyes."

210

We bump across the railroad tracks, and my hands shake from thinking about whether or not I'll do a good job. Nora stops brushing her hair and shoves her head against the seat and closes her eyes. She's older than me, but I bet I can pick as good as she can.

I feel better when the bus speeds up. Now I know I can't chicken out and get off, that I'm really on my way. I wish Nora would open her eyes. I want to tell her about Ellis. About how we were going to build that sailboat and sail around the world. Or buy Swede's Lodge. I want her to know he taught me how to dredge for gold and eat rattlesnake meat. That he's the reason I'm brave enough to be on this bus, going to pick tomatoes. Because he taught me to keep my chin up, to just get busy and pretty soon you can forget to be afraid. And maybe you can forget to be sad, too.

The fields are dewy and have a fusty smell. Sun cracks over the leaves. Nora and I crawl down the rows dragging our empty lugs, watching out for ripe ones. In the rows to our left and right, Mexicans turn the leaves over and pick so fast it makes your head spin. They work in families—moms, dads, and little kids.

"Don't try to go too fast," Nora says, ignoring them. "Pace yourself." She's trying to be nice to me. I close my hands over a big ripe tomato and pull. The skin is tight and dusted with something chalky. It smells better than any tomato I've ever smelled, and feels full and plump when I squeeze.

By ten o'clock Nora and I have each filled four lugs and helped each other drag them back to the start of the row for the trucks to pick them up. The sun is hot already. Gnats buzz my eyes. Nora shrieks whenever she finds a fat, gooey tomato worm.

I think I can't keep picking, but I do. I'm thirsty and my hands ache. I shut my eyes and still see tomatoes and my eyeballs feel like they're burning. When I open my eyes a man in the next row is eating one. Red juice runs down his chin. He wipes it with his long sleeve. All the Mexicans wear long sleeves and hats like it's going to rain.

I pick a tomato for myself and bite. It tastes even better than it feels.

"Oh, puke!" Nora gags. "How can you?" She glares at me over the plants. She's lost her good mood. She's already got a burn and her face is streaked and sweaty.

"It's great, try one." I eat another tomato. The man in the next row looks over at me and smiles.

"Don't smile at him!" Nora hisses.

"Why not?" We're bent down in the row, talking under our arms so he won't hear us.

"You should know why not."

Nora won't sit with the Mexicans at lunch. They stay out in the shade of a tree, but she insists we go eat on the bus. I watch the families from my window. The women's faces are as creased and brown as the men's. They cook beans and tortillas over little stoves, and their teeth show black and crooked when they talk. After lunch the men slouch down and pull their hats over their eyes. The women clean up. Their kids run through the shade chasing a ball.

It goes hot and still. A fly buzzes at the roof of the bus, but he's too stupid to find the open window. I can't stop watching the families.

"Gawd," says Nora when our time is up. "I don't want to go back out there."

212

"I have to," I say. "I only have five lugs. That's just three dollars and seventy-five cents." I've been counting it all morning in my head.

"It's too hot." Nora fans her face with her empty lunch bag. "I'm not going."

The Mexicans are getting up and heading into the fields. Nora stretches her legs out on the seat and rests her head against the window bar. "Wake me when this is over," she says, and yawns.

I stuff my crumpled wax paper into my lunch bag. Outside, the sun weighs a ton. But it's not so bad once I start picking again.

When I finally fill my lug it's too heavy to drag down the row by myself. The Mexican man who smiled at me is watching. He laughs and says something to me in Spanish and I laugh, too.

Then he hops the row between us and picks up the lug and carries it to the end for me. I study his back, how sweat makes flower patterns on the faded checkered cloth. I wonder if he's a father, and how many children he's got. And if he'll carry the rest of my lugs so I can make my ten dollars today, even if ten dollars a day won't be enough.

The Old House

"Do you think we can live here?" Mom asks. We're standing in our old house, where Old Daddy broke down the door.

Live here? My insides get jittery. I didn't even know we still owned this place until today, when Mom told me and Jamie the renters had left. We're here to clean it up.

I look around the living room. I don't remember the plaster walls or the arched hallway opening. But outside the grass is browner than ever.

"It stinks," says Jamie about the chalky air. The renters left a lot of garbage. He kicks a wad of old stuck-together kitchen towels, and when he peels them from the floor the towels stay frozen in their same odd shape.

"Why would we live here?" I say. I can't imagine living on the south side again, putting five people in two rooms and changing all our schools. "If it belongs to us, we should just sell it and put the money into Diamond Street. That's what Ellis would do. Why didn't we just do that before?"

"Cassie's right," says Jamie. "Why didn't we?"

Mom holds her elbows like the room is closing in. "Because we couldn't legally sell it," she says. "We don't own it by ourselves. Sikes owns the other half."

"Dad?" says Jamie like he's choking.

I take a quick breath but don't say anything. I walk under an arch and peer down the hall. I sort of remember the heating grate dusty on the floor. And the way our bedroom looked into the backyard. That's where I used to dream about the fairy who shrank me and flew me out the window glass. All of a sudden I'm a little kid again and I can smell and taste and feel what I used to feel, living here. The feeling only lasts for a second or two, though, before it disappears and my stomach gets queasy.

"Sikes never wanted to sell," Mom is saying when I come back into the living room. "You know. Because we lived here—together. Your dad was so broken up when we divorced …" Mom looks like she's broken up, too, remembering.

"That's crazy," I say. "You've been divorced for years. Maybe he'd sell it now."

"We don't know where he is." Mom looks at me sharp, like I should be more sentimental.

Jamie slumps against a cobwebbed window frame. "How dumb is that?" he says. "To not know where your own father is."

"Where do the rent checks go?" I say.

"God, you sound like Ellis!" Mom shakes her head. "They've been coming to me. But don't get any ideas. They barely pay the taxes and the upkeep."

"Then we need to find him."

"Right. We'll hire a detective," Jamie says.

"I can find him," I say.

Jamie swipes at a cobweb. "Sure you can." He laughs at me.

Confession

Back on Diamond Street, I dig out the wishing-well postcard. The last one Old Daddy ever sent, with his phone number on the back.

"Don't be shocked," I tell Jamie when I hold it out to him.

Jamie just showered. He's still towel-drying his hair and he stops and looks at the postcard. It's yellow and crackled with age, but you can tell who's in the picture. Jamie drops the towel onto his shoulder and takes the worn postcard and turns it over and over in his hands. He stares at Old Daddy by the wishing well. He fingers the words *Wish you were here.* "How did you get this?"

I hate the truth. We're friends again and I don't want to ruin it, but I can't take it back now. "I've had it." I swallow hard. "Since maybe second grade."

He gives me a long, hurt stare.

"He might be gone by now," I rush on, "but I thought if we called the number ... if *I* called the number ..."

Jamie rakes his still-wet hair and water drops hit the postcard like tears.

"I'm sorry," I say. "I was stupid to hide it. I should have shown it to you!"

I try to put my arms around him, but he backs away.

"I was afraid for you to see it. I thought if you found him, you'd go away with him."

His face goes rubbery. "Cassie," he finally says, "what kind of dad just sends a card? What kind of dad?"

"I don't know," I say, surprised. "Aren't you mad at me?"

"It's not your fault." He slaps the wet postcard. "It's his. He's our dad."

My mouth, my eyes, my fingers feel loose and shuddery with the idea that it's not my fault.

"What were *you* supposed to do?" says Jamie.

"Is this Sikes?" I know it is, but I have to ask. I hold the phone tight to my ear.

"Who's this?" Old Daddy says. I thought he'd know my voice.

"It's Cassie."

"Baby Doll!"

The old name makes me raw. Baby Doll, like I'm a horse he can bet on. "Cassie," I say again.

216

Old Daddy laughs. "Cassandra, that's what I named you. Is everything all right?"

I hold the phone even tighter. "You still live at this number," I say. I can hardly believe it.

"Sure I do. Lived here for years. I'm by myself now." His voice drops. "I had to have my old lady committed. She went cuckoo," he says.

You never called us! I listen to him breathing on the other end. I slow my own breath down. I'm four again and afraid. Afraid he'll take Jamie away or forget me at the races or ask me to love him best. It's hard to say it, but I have to. "We need to talk to you. Me and Mom and Jamie."

"You do?" I'm trying to figure out how he sounds. He's not really drunk, but I can't tell if he's sober, either.

"Where do you live? Can you come to River City?"

"Why not? I'm just across town."

"You are?" I feel like I got kicked. All those calls he made with *her* in the background—when the connection sounded so far away—were coming from across the river?

"Cassie?" he says. "What about Ellis?"

Old Daddy

"So sad, too bad, your dad!" Old Daddy hugs me like he's never been away. His chin scratches my chin and he plants a wet kiss on my lips. "You turned out skinny, didn't you?" He pulls off his hat and studies me. He looks shorter and his curly hair is gray. "Where's your mother?"

"She's getting ready."

He drops onto our couch and pulls out his old silver lighter. He clicks it open and the flame pops up. He smokes Kools now instead of Chesterfields. He lights one and places his hat beside him.

"So, how are you, *Cassandra*?"

"I'm in seventh grade. I get A's." It's a funny thing to say. But how can I tell him how I really am? How could I ever explain who I've grown up to be? "No one calls me Cassandra," I add.

"Seventh grade! You know your old man only made it out of grade school? Is Jamie around?"

"He'll be home pretty soon."

"He still dancing?"

"He's going to dance in the Music Circus."

Old Daddy looks impressed. He knows about the Music Circus, a famous performance they hold each year downtown. "He always was a showoff," he says. "Hey, remember that night he danced on the bar?"

The door opens before I can answer, and Nick and Neal run in. They stop when they see Old Daddy. Nick's mitt hangs from his hand. He rubs it along his leg, looking shy. Suddenly the air has been punched from the room.

"Who's this?" Old Daddy asks.

"They're my brothers," I say too loud. "Nick and Neal."

"Oh, Ellis's kids." He tilts his chin and talks while he smokes his Kool.

"My brothers," I say again.

"Good-looking kids," he says as if they weren't here listening. "Sorry to hear about Ellis." He pulls out his money clip and slips two bills from the wad. "This here's for you and Jamie." The old Jacksons. I want to die. How can he just give them to me in front of Nick and Neal? When they don't have a father at all?

Jamie is home. From the living room I hear him talking cautiously to Old Daddy. Jamie's voice is changing, going deeper and solemn, like someone tied a weight to it.

"You didn't say anything, did you?" Mom whispers to me. She's standing over the bathroom sink. She leans toward the mirror and looks into her brown eyes and blinks.

"No. But I don't see why you have to go out with him. Just ask him now." We agreed before Old Daddy came that Mom should be the one to ask about selling the brown-grass house. Now, I'm not so sure.

"I can't just lay that on him!" Mom says. "He'll think that's the only reason we called."

"But it *is* why we called."

"Cassie, he's your father!"

"Ellis was my father."

"Oh, honey. Sikes is your father, too."

"You could have fooled me!" My cheeks feel hot. I flatten against the wall.

"How do I look?" Mom stands back to check more of her reflection. She's letting her hair grow. It's shaped tall on her head with little curls pulled out to rest on her cheeks.

"He would have come around, you know," she says. "It isn't that he didn't want to. It was the circumstances."

I follow as she moves daintily down the hall. Her hips sway and the muscles in her calves tighten. Old Daddy stops talking to Jamie when he sees her. He stands up and takes her arm.

"Where are you going?" I ask.

"How about the old 21 Club, Belle?" he says. He squeezes Mom's arm. He looks at me. "Why? Does it matter?"

"I want to know the phone number. In case."

"That's Cassie," Mom says. "She's always taking down phone numbers."

Old Daddy settles his hat on his head. "I'll look out for her. Don't worry. I was looking out for her before you were born." He gives Mom a sloppy kiss that makes my stomach clench. "See ya, Baby Doll," he says, and they both walk out the door.

"Two hundred dollars!" Mom fans the bills in the air. "Can you believe it? And just in the nick of time. You need clothes. Jamie does, too."

I grab the clock off my nightstand. It says three.

"New pants. New shoes. A dress." She's repeating herself.

"What about the house?"

"That man. Do you know what he did? He left a hundred-dollar bill on the bar."

"He what?"

"He left a hundred-dollar bill!" She plunks onto my bed and sinks against the wall. "Just slapped it down like it was a one and walked off."

"What did you do? Did you get it?"

"I couldn't, honey. The bartender was watching."

"So?" I ball the pillow hard with my fist. "You don't have a job and he's giving away hundred-dollar bills? We could buy food for a month with that!"

"That's your father." She smiles and slumps farther down the wall. "He's always been like that. He used to give away money when he won at the races, too. Just handed out fistfuls to perfect strangers. To anybody with a sob story."

So I didn't imagine it. "What about the house?" I say again.

Mom sighs and shuts her eyes. "Do you want to sleep with me?"

"You didn't ask, did you."

Her eyes pop open. "I asked," she says. Her fingers grab for mine. "Your dad is still such a charm-boy," she says. "A charm-boy. And a bastard."

Revenge

Suddenly Mom is as mad at Old Daddy as she used to be, before they were divorced. "I can't believe him! I can't believe him!" she keeps saying. "He'd rather cry about the past than help us now! I'd like to take a look at where *he's* been living!"

"Let's go, then," Jamie says. Mom is letting Jamie practice driving, since she's had too many beers. I'm in the car with them because we went to the 7-Eleven. In our bag we have milk, toilet paper, and another six-pack.

The six-pack worries me; I won't let her open the beer when Jamie's driving. I like the way he drives, confident, like he knows just what he's doing and has already mapped the streets in his head. He isn't nervous that it's dark and he has to find out how to get across the river. He's mad at Old Daddy, too, but in a different way. A disappointed mad, like when he looked at the wishing-well card and said, *What kind of dad just sends a card?*

But I know Jamie still loves Old Daddy. He's not ashamed of him, like I am.

We find Old Daddy's street. "There it is!" I say from the back seat when Jamie slows the car. The three of us stare at the brick house and ivy-covered porch. The lights are out, as if nobody's home.

We're quiet in the car. We came to do something, but what is there to do? I push at the 7-Eleven bag and Jamie turns around when it rustles.

"Want to TP him?" He grins at me.

"Do you?"

"TP him?" says Mom in her beery voice. She laughs low and wicked and my blood jumps in my veins.

Jamie parks down the street and I hand out the toilet paper. We slip from the car. The yard at the brick house is full of trees. And the grass is black with the trees' stretched shadows. We stand on the edge of the lawn like it's the edge of a cliff. Like there's something we're about to fall into.

It's strange to think I've never seen this house before. His house, where he's lived for years. It looks like a nice place, not for a drunk and a lunatic.

Jamie steps onto the lawn. He throws the first roll. I think of Old Daddy—maybe he's inside after all, maybe he's asleep? I wonder if he'll hear us. I wonder if he'll look out.

Jamie's roll hops into the air and over a tree and comes ribboning down through the leaves. Mom tiptoes across the grass to some shrubs, a white paper stream unraveling behind her. I aim my roll into the tallest tree and let it soar. It sails up clean, holds, and comes down spiraling.

Mom is near the front window now. She strings paper along the shrubs in long swatches, giggling and falling like she's crazy herself. Jamie's loops are growing in his tree, shining from a neighbor's porch light. I toss my own roll again. Other than Mom's giggles and the soft thud of the toilet paper rolls, there isn't a sound.

"Cop!" Jamie hisses. I duck as a patrol car turns the corner, its red light on but not beating. Mom goes on giggling and throwing her roll. Jamie and I run and grab her arms and pull her under the shrubs. "What the hell—" she swears.

The patrol car creeps toward us, its lights catching the strings of paper shuffling on the air. The lawn is damp. We hug together as headlights swing over our backs. My heart drops like a pickax. I want to scream and run but even Mom is frozen. *Freeze tag*, I think. *If you move, you're out.*

The patrol car halts, and a flashlight beam comes on. Shoes on pavement, the static of a police radio. I'm scared now. I don't know what they'll do to us. Is it against the law to TP your own father's house? It was against the law for Old Daddy to break down our door that time, and that was *his* house. What if they think Mom is an unfit mother? What if they take us away?

"Kids," we hear one cop say as the flashlight skids across the lawn. "They must have run off. Somebody's gonna have one hell of a mess in the morning."

The flashlight goes off and the car door thumps shut. The patrol car makes a U-turn.

"They're going away!" Jamie crawls out of the shrubs and watches the taillights retreat. "I thought we were goners."

He heads back over the lawn, picks up his half-finished roll. I help Mom crawl out and we stand there, watching him.

"I just can't believe Sikes said no," Mom says. "I've never asked him for a thing before this."

We run now, breathless. Nothing can catch us. Mom waves

her arms and gets tangled. I grit my teeth to keep from laughing out loud. Jamie and I bump into each other and shriek in great stage whispers. We're having the time of our lives.

It's over too soon. We meet at the edge of the lawn and look back. I can't take my eyes away. I'd like to stay all night, covering Old Daddy's house like a spider spinning a web, or a cook frosting a cake. I'd bury him in white. He'd be snowed in.

The river breeze starts to blow. Maybe it will bring rain. Wet TP is a soggy mess to pick up. Old Daddy will trip around the yard tomorrow, cussing.

Beside me Jamie is in deep shadow. "Well, that's that," he says, and his new weighty voice is sad. We run to the car and Jamie starts it and I turn in the back seat watching Old Daddy's house until I can't see it anymore. The TP sways ghostly in the dark, the brightest thing there. It moves with the wind and lifts and settles. It looks like a celebration. A work of art.

Waking Up

I wake up in the night feeling bad. I've remembered something. Or maybe I dreamed it. About being at the races with Old Daddy. There's a blue uniform and the policeman's bothered face. I'm sitting on a desk and see past the bothered policeman, out the door and into the crowd. Old Daddy's there, walking like the haywire toy. He's holding Jamie's hand and they're heading for the exit.

"Daddy! Daddy!" I yell. "Here I am!" I try to climb off the desk.

"No, you don't!" The policeman holds me back. "Stay put! What's the matter with you? That's not your daddy," he says.

But I was sure it was. I knew my own daddy. How could I not know him when I was meant to love him forever and ever?

Maybe I got it wrong. Maybe I didn't decide not to love him best. Maybe it was Old Daddy who chose. *So sad, too bad, your dad! Tough titty said the kitty when the milk ran dry!* Old Daddy turned around, looked at me, and walked on out the door.

Deed

"Why did you just keep going?"

"What?"

I'm standing on Old Daddy's front porch. It's early morning. He looks shocked to see me when he yanks open the door. He's barefoot. His curly gray hair is piled up crooked with sleep. And his old checkered robe doesn't close right.

"At the races," I say. "When you left me that time. I saw you from the policeman's office. But you just kept on going." My throat squeezes, a big choking hand at it, waiting for him to remember, too.

"What are you talking about? How did you get here?" His eyes are torn blue and skip past me to the toilet-papered lawn. He hits his chin with a fist. "What's this mess?"

"My neighbor drove me." I point out Janet Candy, who waves from her car. "She's going to come back for me in a couple of hours."

"Some damned kids!" Old Daddy's fist raises and shakes.

I feel urgent now. "It was me. I did it. Last night."

"You?" He glares at me like I'm a hatchet murderer. But I have to keep going.

"I came back, though," I say.

He doesn't get it.

"To clean up." I show him my rake and a stack of paper bags. "I don't want to be someone who doesn't come back!"

The wind blows and a looping mess of toilet paper falls onto the porch. He kicks at it. "Didn't I teach you to respect your father?" he shouts. "I always respected my father. No matter what!" He's completely sober this morning. He's not as friendly, sober. "Does your mother know you're here?"

"No." I don't tell him that she and Jamie helped. "And you don't need to shout. I said I'd clean it up." I don't feel urgent anymore. I feel grown up. I start down the brick steps and stop. "Why did you name me Cassandra, anyway?" I say when I turn back.

Old Daddy looks rocky, standing there. "It was your grand-mother's name," he says.

I never knew her. I've never even seen a picture. "You could show me her picture sometime," I say and walk on down to the lawn.

"Where are you going?" Old Daddy says.

"I told you. I'm cleaning up. Then I'm going home."

"Well, is that all you came for?" He grabs his robe belt and cinches it tight.

I start to rake.

"You didn't come about the house?" He frowns and his face is a stony shelf. "What's the deal, anyway?"

"We just need to sell it. For the money." I rake some more. "Or we'll lose our house on Diamond Street."

"Hell's bells," Old Daddy says. "I told her not to run off with that damn cook!"

226

—

We are going to lose our lucky place. Except now I know that the house on Diamond Street is not my lucky place. My lucky place is inside of me, no matter where I live. It's like the day Ellis taught me to shoot the rattlesnake—when I was him and he was me and then he stepped back and I was holding the rifle by myself. He will always be my dad, even if I'm just me again, without him.

I use the rake to pull the toilet paper from the trees. It's hard to reach and my shoulder kinks, jumping up to get it all. I'm raking the soggy TP into piles when Old Daddy comes back outside. He's dressed now, in his salesman suit and shoes. He stands there watching me. Then he shows me an envelope.

"It's the deed," he says. He looks mad again, the way the skin folds down over his torn blue eyes. "It's the last thing your mother and I had together. In *my* name." His hand pats his shirt pocket for his silver lighter.

"Ellis was a good person," I say.

Old Daddy finds his lighter. He doesn't look for a cigarette, though. He just clicks the lighter open and the flame pops up. He holds the flame so close to the deed that I hold my breath. But he isn't going to burn it.

Finally he says, "Well, I guess you turned out all right." And he shoves the envelope at me. "I signed it over. Go on, take it. Before I change my mind." He clicks the lighter shut. "Make sure you get all this up."

I take the envelope slow. I stuff it in my pocket.

Old Daddy shivers like heartbreak. "I didn't see you," he tells me. "That day at the races. I just didn't see you, Baby Doll."

"Okay," I say. I go back to raking. Raking and raking. But the harder I rake, the lighter I feel.

Music Circus

Jamie drapes his body over the crouching body of a beautiful girl. His hands sweep along the sides of her breasts and up to her fingertips. She takes his lead, straightening her own arms and then her body as he brings her upright and looks into her eyes. His face is shining, in love, and when she returns his gaze his heart soars. He grabs her waist and lifts her overhead, lifts her as if she were made of cotton, light as the clouds.

When he sets her down he leaps high and spins, leaps and spins, with powerful grace across the stage. For one instant he nearly disappears, and then, suddenly, he's back, romping from side to side, grinning. This is what love does to him. From elegant suitor to clown. The audience laughs. He pauses, teasing them, making them wait, and in an explosion of movement goes cartwheeling out of sight, no hands.

Jamie says every crowd is different. That each night a different crowd responds to the same performance in a different way. But he's been performing for weeks and all the crowds have loved him. Beside me in the hot canvas tent, Mom wipes her eyes. From the front row his dancing teacher turns around and gives us a thumbs-up. Reece is like Jamie, trim and wound tight as if always ready to spring. Mom says he's happy because all the free lessons he's given Jamie have paid off.

She shoots him a beauty-queen wave, then grabs my hand and squeezes. The charm bracelet on her wrist is the old one, with a charm for each of us kids, our names engraved on the back of a dancer, a silhouette, a fish, and a lamb. It tinkles when she moves.

Mom found a temporary job. She looks so pretty the way she dresses now, her cheeks pink with rouge, and the careful way she has the woman in the beauty parlor broom her hair up into a high red beehive. "He's going to be a star," she cries. "He's going to be a star!" She hugs me and her perfume saturates the muggy air.

Saturday Nights

I've been thinking about it, and I think this is why Ellis took so many moving pictures of us. Because he knew that people come in and out of your life, and a picture fixes them in the moment they reach out to you. When they're all dressed up for a wedding, or putting an arm up in goodbye. You can't really see them reaching in the picture, though, unless you know how to look from the inside. Unless you were there, part of the picture, too, back when it was really happening. Then you can save the memory right, even if, as it turns out, some of the people you love are not in the frame anymore.

Maybe I'll be a photographer one day. Or a filmmaker. I'm always digging out the old movies for Nick, Neal, and Jamie, so we can watch them on Saturday night.

"Who's that?" says Neal. And "Where were we then?" asks Nick. Jamie and I explain each movie to them, so that one day they won't forget.

"That's our old house," Jamie says when we see the brown-grass lawn. "Remember how it looked then, Cass?"

I remember. I'm standing on the porch, and the sunny white cement hurts my eyes. Then Jamie does his heel-toe down the driveway.

We see the Christmas train, and five of us kids riding around and around the living room. Nick and Neal don't remember anything until we get to the gold dredge. Then they remember sliding over the river rocks, and finding gold to make us rich.

I save it for last, the movie of our house in River City, when it was new. There's the little tree tied up with two sticks. After a while Nick and Neal come out in their look-alike sailor suits, stomping by like little men in baggy pants, heading to important places. We run the movies backwards and everybody laughs. And then the picture clacks to a stop and here we still are, all of us together for now, on Diamond Street.